All rights are reserved & retained

by Lakisha Johnson ©2019

Twins Write 2 | Lakisha Johnson

Dedication

This book is for all of you who still live with the pain and voices of the past that has left you, your heart, your self-esteem and your life shattered. I pray you find the strength to recover and be restored.

My Thanks

I must thank God, first, for entrusting me with such an amazing gift. God gives me the stories and I shall give Him my service.

To my entire family, who supports me, THANK YOU!

To each of you who support Lakisha, the author; THANK YOU! I wouldn't be the author I am without readers like you who purchase, download, recommend and review my books. Please, don't stop believing in me.

shat·tered

/ ˈSHadərd /

Adjective

broken into many pieces

exhausted

Eighteen Months Ago

"Oh Camille," my boss, Mr. Townsend calls out when I walk into the office, after a long day in court.

"Yes sir?" I sigh.

"Can you come here for a moment?"

He's waving his hands and has a huge smile.

"I hope it's good news," I mumble, dropping my bags on the chair in my office and walking down the hall. Stepping inside his office, I see the back of the man standing there and it feels like the air is being sucked from my lungs.

"Camille, I want you to speak to someone. You may remember him from law school."

"Yes sir, I remember him," I reply when he sticks out his shaking hand and I grab it. "I'd only hoped he was dead," I say when I'm close enough for only him to hear me.

He quickly releases my hand and looks off.

"Frederick is here consulting on a case with the District Attorney's office," Mr. Townsend says.

"Are you two friends?" I question.

"Oh yes, in fact, Frederick was one of the ones who put you on my radar during your first year of Law School."

"I bet," I say.

"What's that?" Mr. Townsend asks.

"I said, how great. Well, I hope you enjoy Memphis, Professor Frederick. Wait, are you still teaching?"

"No, I haven't taught in years."

I smirk. "If you gentlemen will excuse me, I have some work to finish before I get out of here." I turn around and speed walk back to my office with Mr. Townsend and Stephanie both calling my name. I don't acknowledge either of them. Instead, I walk into my office, close the door and press my back against it.

Why is he here?

"Camille," Stephanie knocks. "Are you okay?"

I take a deep breath and open the door.

"Sorry Stephanie, yes, I'm good. I just needed a minute to catch my breath. What's up?"

"Mr. Townsend is asking if you wanted to join him and his guest for dinner."

"Please tell him no thanks because I have plans already."

I grab my bags and leave. Getting to the car, I take some deep breaths to calm myself but it's not working.

"God, why is he here?"

My hands are shaking as I begin to rock back and forth.

"Calm down Cam," I keep repeating as the tears flood my eyes. I reach over and open the glove box, pulling everything out into the floor. Finally, my hand touches the small bottle of Hennessey. I take it and open it, gulping all of the liquid down.

"You're a virgin?" he asks, smiling.

"I'm going to go because obviously I've given you the wrong idea."

He grabs my arm and pushes me back down on the couch. "You aren't going anywhere."

I start the car and pull out, in search of something stronger and a lot of it to erase the thoughts I'd thought was buried.

*****

I open my eyes but quickly shut them when pain from my head causes me to cringe. I lick my lips because my mouth is dry.

When someone moves beside me, I jump up.

"Ah," I groan before looking at the man lying next to me. "What the f—"

I touch my watch but it's dead. I frantically search for my purse and phone. Finally, finding it on the table, I open it to see it's 4:37 AM and 27 missed calls and texts from Thomas and the girls.

"Shit," I mumble, getting my clothes and staggering into the bathroom.

I throw some water on my face, fix my hair and get dressed. Coming out, the man is still asleep and I don't bother waking him.

Before going home, I search for a 24-Hour Walgreens. I go inside to the pharmacy and purchase a Plan B pill and two bottles of water.

Finally making it home, I'm dreading going in. Turning the corner, I come face to face with Thomas.

"Camille, where have you been?"

"Not now," I tell him pushing pass him.

"Not now? Are you serious? It's after five, in the morning and I've been worried sick. Are you okay? Did something happen?"

"No," I yell, "just leave me alone."

He grabs my arm.

"Don't touch me," I say pushing my back against the wall and squeezing my eyes closed. "Don't," my voice at a whisper.

"What is wrong with you? Camille."

I bolt for the bathroom, slamming the door.

Chapter 1

I walk into Dr. Nelson's office and wait for him to close the door.

"If it's okay with you, I'm in need of Troy, today." I tell him, getting ready to unbutton my shirt.

"No," he sternly says. "What happened between us cannot happen again. It was a mistake."

"Cannot means there's still a possibility, so—"

"No," he says again. "It will not happen again. Now, either you can sit and we talk or you can leave."

"Okay, damn, no need to get your boxers in a bunch," I tell him fixing my clothes and sitting down.

"How are things since you've been home? Has the relationship with your husband gotten any better?"

"No but he'll come around. I'm giving him space to deal with things, his way."

"And what way is that?"

"Giving him space," I say, again, matter-of-factly. "He seems to think I need help so here I am."

"You don't think you do?"

"Do you?"

"Have you had a craving for any drugs?"

"No and I wish you'd stop asking me that. I made a mistake, one freaking time—"

"Twice," he cuts me off.

"I'm not a drug addict. Look, I get that my family and friends are worried about me and I'm sorry for putting them through that but I'm not an addict."

"Then why turn to drugs?"

I shrug.

"Use your words Cam. You're a grown woman who made a choice to use drugs, twice that we know of and I'm pretty sure you know why?"

"Then why don't you tell me, doc. You seem to have all the answers." I scoff.

"Yea but I'm not the one with the issue. Camille, why did you use drugs?"

"Because I could," I yell. "Is that a good enough answer?"

"If that's your truth."

"It is. I used drugs because I could and just like everything else, I thought I'd get away with it but it didn't turn out like I'd thought. Oh well."

"Are you always this self-righteous?"

"I'm confident, Dr. Nelson."

"No, you're delusional if you think you don't have a problem. Cam, you overdosed on a cocktail of cocaine and whatever else. You were in the ICU for days while your family prayed, you'd survive."

"I did survive."

"No, you're alive but this isn't surviving. All you did was get well enough to go right back to your drug or drugs of choice. What's going to happen the next time, you do something like this?"

"I'll plan better," I smile.

"Why are you here?"

"I thought it was for the sex but I guess it's because my insurance pays for it."

"Camille—"

"It's Cam," I correct.

"Camille, I apologize for crossing the line with you. I never should have allowed things to get as far as they did. For that reason, I think it best, I refer you to another doctor."

"Whatever," I say. "Are we done?"

"This isn't helping you and you really need help," he states, "and if you continue with these sessions, you've got to promise to put forth an effort."

"I have been putting forth an effort, by showing up."

"That's not what I mean," he sighs. "There are some things you need to deal with, things you've probably suppressed and maybe the drugs and the sex is a way to cope but—"

"I haven't suppressed anything because there's nothing wrong with me. I wasn't molested by my father, raised by a crack head or bullied in school. My mother is an attorney and my father, a judge. I'm an only child and they raised me well. I'm good and there's nothing wrong with having a good time."

"Is that what you call the things you've experienced? Going on a drug induced binge that had you missing for over 24 hours?"

"I wasn't missing, I was orgasming," I laugh.

"This isn't a joke, it's your life and almost overdosing and being in the hospital for seven days, isn't a good time. Camille, you can continue to act like this isn't a big deal but it is."

"Are we done because I need to get out of here?"

"We're done whenever you say we are."

"Fine," I say getting up. "We're done."

"Camille, if you decide to continue this journey, take some time to journal the thoughts that were going through your mind before the overdose. Maybe we can dissect them on your next visit."

"My next visit? Didn't you say, you were going to refer me to a different doctor or that this can be done when I say and I said it? Damn doc, I don't know who needs help more, me or you."

"I know what I said but you really need this, Camille. Please, let me help you."

"I'll think about it," I say walking out.

Chapter 2

I walk into Chloe's house for our girl's night.

"Who said no?" I question, strolling in.

"Well, if you don't look all Cam like with this damn dress on for girl's night," Ray laughs and I twirl.

"Girl whenever I get the chance to get out the house and away from Thomas gloomy ass, I'm going to dress up. Now, who said no to something."

We all look at each other.

"What? One of you bitches better tell me what's going on."

Lyn sighs. "The night you overdosed; I was attacked and raped, at my store."

I stand there, listening to Lyn talk and the more she talks, the more tears fill my eyes.

"You were raped and didn't tell me?"

"You were in no condition to help, boo."

"Cam, why are you crying?"

"Because I wasn't there. Damn it! My selfishness caused me to be away from you all when you needed me and I'm sorry."

"Girl, hush because you were in no shape to help us. Hell, we could barely help ourselves," Ray tells me.

"What else have I missed?"

They look at each other again.

"Well," Lyn says, "Justin is gay, Chloe is divorced and pregnant by Todd, Mike is in rehab, Brian is sick and Paul has a whole other family." She blurts everything without taking a breath. "Did I miss anything, ladies?"

They all shake their heads.

"What kind of flip, flopping, foolishness is going on here? Damn, I can't even go in a coma without all hell breaking loose," I tell them. "I don't even know what to say."

"How do you think we feel?"

"I need a bottle of wine."

"What did I miss?" Chloe asks, walking in.

"Really Chloe?" Kerri laughs.

"What? I was talking to Todd," she says with a smirk.

"Hmm, so what's going on with you and Chef French?" Ray asks looking her up and down.

"Nothing, well, I don't know. He wants to get to know each other before the baby comes."

"That's what's up," I say and they look at me. "What? I think it's cool that he's willing to get to know you, for you and not just as his baby's mother. This is his baby, right? You wouldn't be lying to that man, would you?"

"Hell no. I probably would have lied to Chris' pitiful ass because I can't see myself raising anything with him but not to Todd. This is his baby."

"Aite because I'll sign you up for Maury," I add.

"While you're all up in people's business, what's up with you? We haven't had a chance to really get together and talk since everything happened."

"Can we eat first?" Kerri asks.

We fix our plates and drinks before moving into the living room. We spend the next hour eating, drinking and laughing. After cleaning the kitchen, we go back and get settled.

Lyn tells us about moving out and Kelsey knowing about Paul's affair.

My phone vibrates with a text from Mr. Prosecutor.

HIM: It really was good seeing you.

"Maybe we should get Cam's therapist number," Kerri says. "It looks like we can all use the help."

"Camille, you are still getting help, right?"

"Hello, earth to Cam."

"What did you say?" I ask, confused.

"If you'd get out of that phone, you can hear us."

"Whatever repeat what you said," I tell Kerri while locking my phone and putting it in my lap.

"I asked if you were still getting help."

"Define help," I state, sipping my wine.

"As in therapy, talking to someone and actually listening?"

"Yea, I've been a few times."

"But?"

"But it's not for me. I don't like folk all up in my business," I reply.

Chloe touches my hand. "Cam, I love you sweetie but we all know, therapy won't do you any good unless you go for you."

"I don't need therapy. Therapy is for people with real problems."

"Real problems," Shelby repeats, "and yours aren't? Camille, you overdosed and was in the hospital for over a week. Not to mention the dialysis."

"Shelby, please don't start preaching," I exhale. "The night I overdosed, Thomas and I had a huge fight and he put me out. He literally packed my bags and kicked me out. He was right to do it because I was spiraling and I didn't realize how bad it was but I didn't intentionally set out to overdose.

I thought I could control everything, like I've always done but I couldn't. That night when I got home, he gave me an ultimatum to either get help or leave and being me, I said—"

"I don't need help," they all say.

"I don't. Yes, I messed up but when I left the house, I was angry and none of you would answer my calls. I don't blame y'all though because, after LA, I wouldn't have answered my calls, either. Anyway, I was pissed and in, F the world mode.

I stopped at a liquor store and drove until I ended up at a motel. There was a young lady there who came to my room, because I was screaming and talking to myself. At first, I refused her but when she said she had something to make me forget my problems, I jumped at the chance. I had no idea what she gave me but after a minute, I guess I got what I'd been wishing for, to quiet the thoughts in my head."

"God has a way of getting our attention, doesn't He?" Ray questions. "Look at all we've endured;

these last few months. Divorce, sickness, attacks; hell, you name it. Pastor Reeves said something when she was at the hospital that day. Hold on," she gets her phone. "She said, God is allowing each of you to suffer differently yet at the same time. Please do not curse this test as it'll be what's needed to strengthen you and your faith."

"Amen to that but can we change the subject to something else, less draining?" I inquire.

"I got something," Ray says. "I was going through a box of old stuff when I was packing Justin's stuff. Do y'all remember the time, after we'd been at TSU for a week and Cam got caught by campus police, having sex on the football field and we had to go and bail her out?"

I watch, in pure terror as she reaches into her pocket and pull out an old polaroid picture.

"Oh my God, Raylan Greer, no you didn't!" I scream, snatching it from her. "Oh my God, I remember this but it wasn't my fault because I told, I think his name was James, not to let his pants drop.

He did and when the cops showed up, he couldn't even get off me. I was so mad."

We all burst into laughter until Lyn gets quiet.

"Lyn, are you okay?"

She begins talking about her problems which then leads Shelby to vent. I roll my eyes because I thought this was supposed to be girl's night and not waiting to exhale. *Shit!*

I'm refilling my wine glass, for the third time when I hear Shelby's voice get louder.

"Kerri when did Brian tell you he was sick?"

"Let me explain Shelby," Kerri stammers.

"I'm all ears."

"Oh shit," I say sipping wine when I walk back into the room.

I'm looking from Kerri to Shelby as she goes into detail about her meeting with Brian. Then she starts to tell about how she knows Brian, from junior high school.

I'm sipping my wine and looking from one to the other.

"Did y'all sleep together?" Shelby inquires.

"Shelby, I'm sorry I didn't tell you but I begged him to and he promised he would."

"You still didn't answer the question. Did you and my husband ever have sex?"

"One time, before he was your husband because again, we were fifteen."

"Wow," Shelby says.

"It's not a big deal. I knew him, years before you met. We went to school together and out on a few, childhood dates that's it. The sex, between us, didn't really count because it was both of our first times."

"Kerri, learn when to shut up," I state but they continue to go back and forth until Chloe cries out in pain.

"Aw hell, y'all done sent the damn girl into labor."

Chapter 3

Our girl's night ended early with Chloe spending the night in the hospital and since I wasn't ready to go home, I drive around before pulling into the parking lot of Chicks and Cigars, a new cigar bar.

I sit for a minute trying to decide if I want to go inside or find something more interesting to get inside of me. I have to laugh at my own thoughts.

Opening my contacts, I scroll to one name and then another until I hear the girl's voices in my head saying, "Cam, take your ass home."

"Forget y'all," I say out loud turning off the car, grabbing my purse, phone and getting out.

Walking inside, there is a live band and a fairly nice size crowd. I go into the humidor room to find a cigar. Cigar smoking isn't something I do, regularly but I've enjoyed it ever since Judge Alton turned me on to it. There's nothing like having a good cigar and drink to mellow you out.

After finding my cigar of choice, I make my way to the end of the bar.

"What can I get you?" the bartender asks, stopping when she recognizes me. "C," she sings, "girl, where have you been?"

"Paige, oh my God," I reach over the bar to give her a hug. "I've been busy and I guess that's why I didn't know you were back in Memphis."

"I'm surprised Charles didn't tell you but I've been back about six months. Anyway, we'll have to catch up. What are you having?"

"Hennessy Black with ginger ale," I tell her as she hands me a cutter, torch lighter and ashtray; rubbing my hand as she sits them in front of me.

"Is this seat taken?"

I smile when I look up to see Charles or rather, Judge Alton standing there.

"Judge, fancy meeting you here."

"Camille, I thought that was you. How are you?" he questions giving me a hug. "I've missed seeing you at the courthouse."

"I'm good and I'll be back and giving you hell in no time. How have things been?"

"You know, the same. With the crime in Memphis, there is never a dull moment."

"Are you here alone?" I inquire.

"No, I'm with some friends. Would you like to join us?"

"No thanks. I'm not staying long."

"Well, if you change your mind we're over in the corner. It was really good to see you."

"You too, Judge."

I watch him walk away before licking my lips. Paige sits my drink down as my phone vibrates with a text from Thomas.

THOMAS: Where are you?

ME: Hello to you too. I'm at Chicks and Cigars. Would you like to join me?

THOMAS: Wow, I'm surprised you didn't lie again.

ME: Again?

THOMAS: I thought you were at Chloe's for a "girl's night."

I roll my eyes at his use of quotations around girl's night.

ME: How did you know I wasn't?

THOMAS: I drove by and didn't see any cars.

ME: WOW! First, I don't need you checking on me. I'm not a child. Second, Chloe got sick and is staying overnight in the hospital. Third, I'M MFKIN GROWN!

THOMAS: I'm aware but I also know what grown Camille does.

"I'm not about to do this." I mouth to myself, putting my phone on do not disturb and over into my purse.

For the next hour, I smoke my cigar and enjoy the music and drinks. I pay my tab and head to the bathroom. When I'm done, I walk out but is pulled into a dark corner.

A warm mouth covers mine.

"Hmm. Did you really think I'd let you leave without tasting you?"

I smile. "I'm flattered but I can't, not tonight," I tell her.

"Come on C, you know it's been a while."

"I know babe but I've got to get home."

She whines.

"I'll make it up to you, next time."

I silently curse myself for turning that licking down but I'm tired. Fifteen minutes later, I'm home. I turn the alarm off and back on before heading to the guest room where I'm still staying. Coming out of the bathroom, after a shower, I jump at Thomas sitting there.

"I'm surprised you came home," he sarcastically says. "I thought you'd be somewhere sleeping with somebody else's husband or wife, for that matter because that's what the great Camille Shannon does."

"Are you drunk?" I inquire.

"Are you?"

"Thomas, I am not in the mood to entertain your insecurities. I'm tired and going to bed. Please close the door behind you on the way out."

"Did you sleep with someone tonight?"

"Really?" I laugh. "No but to be honest I wanted too. You know why? Because it's been months since my husband or anybody has touched me, for that matter. I told you, I was working on me and I am. That's why when I was propositioned tonight, I turned it down.

Only to come home to this freaking guest room, horny as hell. Oh but the next time I'll go on and cheat since you're going to accuse me, anyway."

"Why am I not enough for you?"

"Thomas, please leave."

"I miss you," he blurts. "I miss you but I don't trust you."

"If you miss me then say that but I will not continue to apologize for the past. I messed up and you don't trust me. I KNOW," I yell. "I know because you won't let me forget."

"I'm trying."

"No, you're not because if you were trying we'd be working together to fix our marriage. What you're doing is trying to control me. Thomas, I'm sorry I hurt you but I can't make you trust me and if we're going to argue each time I leave here; then maybe it's time I find my own place."

"Damn it, Camille," he says moving quickly to kiss me. He backs me into the wall and kisses me so passionately that I'm scared to move. "I've missed you." He kisses my neck, my chest and then my breast.

I push him back. "Wait, are you sure this is what you want because I—"

He smacks my hand away, snatches my gown over my head and kicks my legs open.

"At this very moment I want my wife. We'll deal with everything else, tomorrow."

With that, I slide his pajama pants down and wrap my hands around his neck. He picks me up, carrying me over to the bed where he lays me at the edge.

"Oh," I moan as he moves to the one spot, he knows all too well. It doesn't take long before he's entering me. I open my eyes to find him looking at me. I pull him closer wrapping my legs around him as our lips touch.

When we're done, he grabs his pajama pants and storms out the room.

"Well, goodnight to you too."

Chapter 4

Three Months Later

I'm sitting on the side of the bed as thoughts from the previous months invade my mind. One minute, we're having girl's night at Chloe's and the next, chaos and confusion.

Brian dies from a seizure, he should have survived and the same night, Chloe has the baby early. We thought Lyn was doing good until I found her in an empty apartment, contemplating leaving the country and I had to threaten her with bodily harm.

Kerri and Mike are working on things and Ray, well she's still trying to figure shit out. Thomas, he's still being an asshole and I'm still in this freaking guest room.

Mane, it's been a hell of a life lesson that's for sure.

I guess things are finally at a place of settling down since the holidays are over and I'm officially going back to work. I talked to Shelby, last night and she seems to be doing better; with each passing day. As for me, I'm coping with the circumstances of my actions.

At least, I think I am.

"Good morning," Thomas says walking up behind me at the kitchen counter.

"Good morning, Mr. Shannon."

"I love you," he tells me.

I turn around to look at him.

"What?" he asks.

"I love you too," I stammer "but it's been a while since I've heard you tell me that."

"I know but with everything that happened with Brian," he pauses "that could have been me."

"Thomas—"

"No, let me finish. I realized just how close I was to losing you yet God allowed you to recover and now, I think it's time for us to be restored."

"Really?"

"Yea. You've been going to therapy and over the last couple of months, you've changed. I just want us to be happy again."

"I want that too."

He kisses me and I begin to pull his shirt out of his pants. "Make love to me."

He kisses me again but steps back. "I will tonight but I have to go. I got court at nine."

"Thomas—"

"I promise, I'll give you all of big daddy, tonight when you move back into our bedroom."

He kisses me again, grabs his briefcase and walks out, pushing his shirt into his pants.

I throw my coffee cup into the sink.

*****

"Mrs. Shannon, Judge Alton would like to see you before you leave." I finish packing up my computer and files before grabbing all my things and walking to Judge Alton's office.

"Hey," he says when I walk in, "welcome back. I was glad to see you on my docket again."

"Why, did you miss me?" I ask smiling.

"Of course, you know I can never get enough of your smart-ass mouth," he says closing the door. "But seriously, how are you? I haven't seen you since that night at the cigar bar and you're looking very good, by the way."

"Thank you and I am doing very well. Glad to be back at work."

"Hmm, how can you still smell this sweet after being in court all day?" he kisses my neck.

"Is this why you needed to see me?" I ask laughing.

"Yea," he replies in between kisses before grabbing my hand and placing it between his legs.

I close my eyes, squeezing him. "I can't do this," I tell him, barely above a whisper. "I'm trying to repair my marriage and I can't do that bent over your desk."

He steps back. "I'm sorry. I never want to be the reason your marriage doesn't work."

"I know and you don't have to apologize. I should have told you when I walked in." I can't even make eye contact with him, for looking at the bulge in his pants. "Damn it." I move from the desk and begin pacing. "I need to get out of here."

"Wait, I'm sorry."

"No, you didn't know but thank you for respecting me enough not to push."

"Always," he says fixing his pants. "Where are you headed? Care to join me for a cigar and drink?"

"No thanks. I'm going to stop by and check on my friend Shelby then head home."

"She's the one whose husband passed? How is she doing?"

"She's getting better, taking it a day at a time. Losing a spouse is a hard pill because it changes the total dynamic of your life."

"I know," he sighs. "It's been three years for me and sometimes it feels like yesterday. Please let her know she's in my prayers."

"I will," I grab my things, "thanks for the meeting. I'll see you later."

I open the door and walk out, only to run into Thomas.

"Camille where are you coming from?"

"I just finished up a case and needed to talk to Judge Alton about something."

He looks back at the door. "Is that all you were doing?"

"Wait, are you serious?"

He moves closer to me. "Is this because I wouldn't have sex with you this morning."

"Wow, are we really doing this? I thought we'd moved pass this?"

"Have we, Camille?" he questions looking me up and down.

"Nothing happened, we were only talking. You can go and ask him yourself. Better yet, you want to smell my pus—"

"That's enough," he says grabbing my hand and looking around when I go to raise my skirt.

"No, this is enough. You were talking all that shit about restoration this morning and now, not even eight hours later, you're accusing me."

"Whatever Camille, I was only asking."

"No, you were accusing. Am I going to have to explain every time you see me with a man? If so, I can't do this."

"Can we talk about this when we get home?"

"No, I'm talked out. Don't wait up."

Chapter 5

Music playing

> *"Oh, come on and rock me, ooh, girl*
>
> *Oh, come on and rock me, ooh, girl*
>
> *Hey, girl, long time no see*
>
> *Do you have a little time to spend with me?*
>
> *I wanna know what's been going on*
>
> *In your life, huh, talk to me, baby"*

"Paige," I call out when I don't see her in the living room.

"Hey, I didn't hear you come in," she smiles.

"That's because you got this Freddie Jackson bumping. What do you know about that?"

"I know enough," she says pulling me to her. "I was glad you finally took me up on my offer."

"Is that so? Why don't you show me then," I say pushing her away and pulling my shirt over my head, while we're walking to the bedroom, leaving a trail of clothes.

When we get to her bedroom, she pushes me down on the bed.

"Close your eyes and don't say one word."

"Now—"

She grabs my mouth, "not a word Camille," she orders.

I lay back and close my eyes until I feel something around my wrist. My eyes pop open.

"No," I say, shaking my head. "I don't like to be tied up."

"That's because you like to be in control but not tonight. Now, be a big girl and play along."

"No, untie me. UNTIE ME!"

"Okay, hold on."

She snatches the scarves from my wrists and I get off the bed.

"What's wrong?" she questions as I rush out the room, grabbing my clothes. "Camille."

I don't answer while I quickly get dressed.

"I'm sorry, it's just scarves," she explains.

"I have to go," I stutter. "I'm sorry but I have to go."

I rush out of the house and into my car. I throw my purse and shoes over into the passenger seat before starting the car and pulling off.

My hands are shaking.

"Damn it," I scream hitting the steering wheel.

*****

"I DON'T NEED NO FREAKING HELP! THERE IS NOTHING WRONG WITH ME!"

"That's what all addicts say. Can't you see that you're damaged? This isn't even about our vows anymore because there is something wrong with you. Whatever it is, happened over a year ago. Please, just let me help you."

I jump when I hear Dr. Nelson call my name. I grab my purse and follow him into his office.

"Camille, are you okay?" Dr. Nelson asks, closing the door. "Where were you, just then?"

"What do you mean?" I ask, looking confused.

"You looked like you were deep in thought. Did something happen?"

"No, I'm good."

"Are you sure?"

"Yes," I snap at him. "I'm fine, Dr. Nelson but I am sick of people asking me that."

"Hmm," he says.

"What is that for?"

"Camille, you've been coming here, for almost five months. When are you going to face the reality of your situation?"

"Here we go," I sigh, rolling my eyes. "Look doc, you need to make up your mind who you want to be. One minute you're Dr. Nelson with all this get help crap and the next, you're Troy who likes his nipples sucked. Who are you today so I'll know?"

"You're right and for that I'm sorry. Camille, from our first meeting, at the hospital, I've failed you."

"You failed me?" I laugh. "What am I, a science project? How about this? Let's end these sessions and go on about our lives because they aren't doing a bit of good, anyway."

"That's because you aren't taking this serious."

I laugh, again, harder. "And you are? Dude, we had sex, during our second session and the only reason we stopped, before, is because I put an end to it. So, spare me this bullshit. If you really wanted me to take this seriously, you would have ended our "agreement,"" I put in air quotes, "a long time ago."

He sighs. "Camille, like I've stated, I'm sorry for my actions because I realize they've only added to your problem."

"I don't have a problem."

"And the only way you can truly get the help you need; we have to we end these sessions," he states, ignoring my statement.

"Finally, we agree on something."

We both get up. I bend down to get my purse and when he opens the door, motioning for someone to come in; I stand up straight.

"Camille this is Dr. Melody Scott."

"And?"

"And she is going to take over your therapy sessions from now on."

"Negro, didn't we just agree to end this façade?"

"No, we agreed to end your sessions with me but Camille, you do need help."

"No, what I need is for all you motherfuckers to stop judging me. I'm out."

"Please wait," she says. "Dr. Nelson only asked me to come so that I can help you. Will you, at least give it a try, for real this time?"

"For real, this time? Lady, you don't know me."

"I may not know you, personally but I know your type," she states, looking me up and down.

I chuckle. "My type?"

"Yes, you're a woman who, on the outside, is well put together. You have your Steve Madden heels, your pencil skirt and cute blouse with your hair always done and your smart mouth. You graduated at the top of your class and I'm willing to bet, you rarely lose but inside, you're shattered.

Something happened that left you so scarred that this persona, the one we're witnessing, was created to mask it all. The sad part, you know you need help but you're afraid of admitting the very thing that damaged you. Why? I'm not here to judge you, Camille but I am here to help you be restored."

"Wow," I say slowly clapping. "Girl, you almost had me but I don't need to be restored because I'm good with all my broken pieces. Actually, I'm better than good but thanks for the speech. You're really good at it."

"Is that why you cry yourself to sleep, some nights or question why God wasn't there, for you?"

"You don't know me," I say getting closer to her.

"Sweetie this tough act may scare someone else but not me. If you change your mind and when you're ready to deal with whatever has shattered the real Camille Shannon, I'll be here."

I brush pass them and out of the office. Getting to the car, I throw my purse into the passenger seat before gripping the steering wheel.

"She doesn't know me," I seethe, "and I don't need no help. Not from her and certainly not from God."

Chapter 6

"Oh, you're a feisty little bitch," he smiles. "I like that but I suggest you shut up and be a big girl."

"Please don't do this."

"You don't know when to shut up, do you? Get on your knees."

"NO!"

He snatches me by the hair.

"Get on your knees because tonight, I'm in control and you're going to learn how to play along."

I bolt up from the bed, looking around. I relax when I realize, it wasn't real. I touch my face and realize I was crying.

I throw the covers back and swing my leg over the side of the bed. Seeing the sheet of paper, Ray gave me, laying on the nightstand, I pick it up. It's her notes from a prayer conference at their church. They invited me to go but me and God aren't there yet.

She highlighted a scripture.

"Psalm 34, verses 18 through 20," I say out loud. *"The LORD is close to the brokenhearted; he rescues those whose spirits are crushed. The righteous person faces many troubles but the LORD comes to the rescue each time. For the LORD protects the bones of the righteous; not one of them is broken!"*

I lay the paper back down.

"I wish that were true," I mumble before going into the bathroom. "Where we you when I was being broken and my heart shattered like glass. Huh God? You're supposed to be there for your children but where were you? Hello, I'm listening. Just like I thought, you never answer."

I walk into the bathroom, turning the water on, in the shower before undressing and stepping under the water.

"If you change your mind and when you're ready to deal with whatever has shattered the real Camille Shannon, I'll be here."

"I don't need no freaking help," I yell.

"Camille? Are you okay?"

"Not now, Thomas."

"Do you need help?" he asks again.

I angrily turn off the water and get out the shower, snatching the door to the bathroom open. He jumps back.

"Do I need help? If I did, you wouldn't be the one I'd call. Hell, you keep toying with my emotions. Telling me you miss me, you love me, you want me back in our bedroom and then with the same mouth, you accuse me. I can't keep doing this."

He steps towards me and I step back.

"No," I say, trying not to cry. "Thomas, I can't do this anymore. I'm exhausted from the constant back and forth that's getting us nowhere. It seems, the more I try, the more you turn away from me when I'm doing what I said I'd do. I'm going to therapy and

I'm being the wife, you said you wanted; all from this guestroom. I don't know what else to do. So, please just leave me alone."

"I invited you back to our bed," he says.

"Inviting me back to our bed is totally different than inviting me back to our marriage. Just go and leave me alone."

"I'll leave you alone and when you're ready, we can talk about this." He turns to walk out but stops. "Are we still going to dinner at Shelby's?"

"Wow. I should have known there was another reason you came in here. You act like you actually cared but it was only to find out if I'm still going to dinner? Hell no. I'm not going to some dinner to act like we're happily married."

"Please Camille, it's Valentine's Day?"

"And that means what? Are we supposed to act happy? Negro please. You can take Valentine's Day and shove it up your—"

"Fine," he says aggravated. "You act like all our problems can be solved in a day. It takes time to fix broken vows but can we start somewhere?"

"Sure."

He smiles.

"Start with your ass being on the other side of this door and out of my face."

*****

"Camille, thank you for doing this tonight." Thomas says reaching over to grab my hand when we pull up to Shelby's house.

I move before he can touch me. "I'm not doing this for you. I'm doing this for Shelby because she begged me to come. Otherwise, I would have been at home."

I get out, slam the car door and walk into the house.

"No, I've been so busy with trying to get Brian's affairs in order that I haven't had a chance to reach out to anybody, hardly." I hear Shelby say.

"Me either," Ray adds, "but maybe Cam has—"

"Maybe Cam has what?" I ask, walking in on the end of their conversation.

"Spoken to Lyn."

"Hold that thought," I tell them when I see a fine piece of man, out of my peripheral view. "Gul, I know that ain't Brock."

"Yea," they both say.

"Damn, that boy done grewed the hell up."

"Did this fool just say grewed?" Ray asks as we laugh.

"Baby, I remember the last time he was here and he didn't look nothing like that. Damn."

"Calm down Blanche from Golden Girls, that man is married."

"If that's his wife, beside him, I'll do her too."

"Girl, what happened to you turning over a new leaf?" Kerri inquires.

"I turned the MF-er back. Y'all look, I've tried to make my marriage work. I promised Thomas I'd get help and I have. I've been doing counseling and I only did the counselor, once."

"Bitch," Ray shakes her head.

"What? Hell, I had to take baby steps. Anyway, after him and one time with the prosecutor; I cut everybody off and started taking therapy, half way serious. You know what that got me?

A dry coochie and the 3rd degree from Thomas every time he sees me talking to a man. I'm sorry y'all but if this is the way life is going to be, I may as well cheat. At least, I'll be happy."

"Wait, you ain't had no sex from Thomas?" Ray and Shelby both ask, at the same time, whispering.

"Once and it was a wham bam, thank you ma'am; on his part, not mine," I say when Thomas walks in. "Ugh, here his judgmental ass come."

We all try to keep from laughing.

"Shelby, Ray and Kerri, it's nice to see you ladies. Happy Valentine's Day."

"Hey Thomas and Happy Valentine's Day to you. There's liquor on the bar and appetizers in the kitchen. I'll be right back." Shelby states.

I follow her into the kitchen. "Shelby—what the hell? Chelle?"

"Hi," she smiles. "I didn't know you were going to be here."

"Girl, I almost didn't recognize you with clothes on. How have you been?"

"Great, actually. I'm a full-time chef now and business has been great," she beams.

"I bet."

"No," she laughs, "not like that. I don't do that anymore. I have an investor who helped me start my business so I wouldn't have to do that part of it."

"That's great. Well, the food smells wonderful and you look good."

I grab Shelby's arm, pulling her out of the kitchen.

"How in the fuck did you find her, out of all the chefs in Memphis?"

"You shared her information on Facebook and since you don't post regularly when I went to your page and saw that she was running a Valentine special, I booked her. What's the big deal?"

"She's the one we had the threesome with."

Her mouth forms into an O.

"What are y'all whispering about?" Thomas asks, walking up on our conversation.

"Shelby's choice of chefs, for the night. Why don't you go and see who it is?"

When he walks around the corner, she and I burst into laughter when Chloe, Todd and the baby come in.

"Girl, you're going to hell," she tells me and I shrug.

I let her go and walk back into the kitchen and Thomas abruptly stops talking.

"Uh, what's going on?" I ask looking from him to her. "Why did you stop talking?"

"We didn't. We were talking about the menu and Valentine's Day."

"Oh, is that all because it looks like I intervened on a personal conversation. Is there something I'm missing?"

"Camille, don't start anything because there's nothing going on." Thomas says huffing like I'm getting on his nerves.

"Hold on boo because —"

"Everybody is here so we can eat," I hear Shelby say.

"Let's eat," he says turning me around and leading me to the dining room.

"What's going on with you and her?"

"Nothing."

"Nigga, if you think for a moment, I believe that, you're crazy. Don't worry though, I won't say anything tonight but I will find out."

Chapter 7

After dinner, we're headed out to Shelby's patio, for drinks when I excuse myself and go to the bathroom. I'm standing at the sink washing my hands when the door burst open.

"Oh shi—I'm sorry, I didn't realize anyone was in here. The door was unlocked."

I look him up and down.

"What's up Brock?"

"Hey Cam, sorry, I have ice cream on my hands or I'd give you a hug."

"It's cool but let me get out of here because I'd hate for you to get in trouble with the wife."

"I can say the same for you. Things seem a little tense with the husband."

"Forget him."

"You still ain't changed," he smirks. "Still the Cam I remember."

"What could you possibly remember about me when it's been years?"

He walks closer to me, leaning into my ear. "I remember you being as wet and sweet as this ice cream."

"Well, sucks for you because things have definitely changed."

"How so?" he asks, moving to the sink.

"I'm wetter and sweeter."

I turn to walk off.

"We should get drinks and catch up."

I smile before turning back to him.

"We should. Here," I take my phone from my shirt and hand it to him after he dries his hands, "put your number in and I'll shoot you a text. Hit me up when you're ready."

Instead of taking the phone, he pulls me into the bathroom and closes the door. Pressing me against the wall, he slides his hand into my tights. I raise my leg to give him access.

He pushes harder and I grip his shirt, biting my lip as my orgasm peaks.

"Damn," he moans and I close my eyes, moving against his hand before pushing him back. He licks his fingers. "You need to get out of here," he growls and I lick his lips.

I smile before cracking the door to look out.

Coming into the kitchen, I roll my eyes when Thomas is standing there.

"You okay?"

"Much better now, thanks."

*****

"Hey Stephanie," I say a few days later, walking into the office.

"Good morning Camille, how was your Valentine's Day?"

"Eventful, what about yours?"

"Well," she sings holding out her hand. "Raymond finally proposed."

"Congratulations. I am so happy for you."

"Thank you," she smiles. "I loaded your schedule to your iPad and you have a new client coming in at eleven."

"The new client, is it—"

"Monica Walker, who wants to talk about her father's company," she finishes my statement.

"Got it. Can you pull the files so I can be ready when she gets here?"

"Yes ma'am, I'll bring them right in."

I walk into my office and drop my bag, on the desk. I sit in my chair and begin to play back last night with Thomas and Chelle. I grab my computer to do some research on Chelle but Stephanie comes in.

"Here's the file but Mr. Townsend would like to see you in his office."

"Did he say the reason?"

"No ma'am."

"Ok. Thanks Stephanie."

I jot a note, on my notepad before pushing away from the desk to meet with the head of our firm, Mr. Milton Townsend.

"Mr. Townsend, you wanted to see me?" I say pushing his door open to see Judge Alton sitting in his office.

"Yes, come in. You know Judge Charles Alton, don't you?"

"I do," I remark.

"Yes, I've had the privilege of having her, in my courtroom," Charles says smiling.

"It's good to see you again Judge," I say giving him a sly look. "What can I do for you gentleman this morning?"

"Have a seat. Do you want anything to drink?"

"No, I'm fine."

"Camille, a pressing matter has come to our attention and we have to move on it quickly."

"Okay, is it a case?"

"Not a case but do you know Judge Sumner?"

"From District Seven? Yes, I've heard of her but haven't been in her courtroom. Why?"

"She has terminal cancer and won't be able to handle the term she was just voted into."

"I'm so sorry to hear that but what does she need from us?"

"It's not what she needs, rather what is about to happen?"

"I don't follow," I say to them.

"Your name has been recommended as a candidate to fill her seat," Mr. Townsend says.

"Wait, what?"

"Camille, you're a great attorney, as it's evident by your work. Mr. Townsend and I, both agree that you'd make a damn good judge." Judge Alton adds.

"Uh," I say sitting back in my chair, "wow, this is not what I was expecting when I walked in here. Wow."

"I know this is a shock but when the opportunity presented itself, we knew we had to act. This is a great opportunity."

"Yes sir, it is and it's one I've been preparing for since I was little."

"Then why aren't you excited?"

"I am but I'm also in shock because I thought I'd have a few more years to prepare for it."

"God's plans always outweigh our plans," Mr. Townsend remarks.

"God's plans," I whisper.

"Look Camille, if we didn't think you were ready for this, we wouldn't be having this conversation. However, you are and that's why your name has been given to the Tennessee Judicial Nominating Committee as a candidate. All you have to do is fill this questionnaire out," Mr. Townsend says handing me a packet.

"And that's it?"

"Once you fill out the questionnaire, the judicial committee will go through a detailed process to select three names from the pool of candidates. It can take a few weeks but then, they'll submit their choices to the governor. He then has 60 days to decide the best person to fill the seat."

"Wow, I—I, uh, I don't know what to say."

"Camille, we believe you are the best woman to replace Judge Sumner. This open seat is in your district and you're more than qualified for it. Yes, it came a few years early but don't allow fear to keep you out of purpose."

I get up from my chair. "This is an amazing opportunity and it would be crazy for me to pass on it but how long do I have before I need to give this back?"

"A week at best," Judge Alton answers.

"Then there'll be sixty days before a decision is made, right?"

"First, there is a decision made, narrowing down the pool to three. Then, the names are submitted to the Governor, who then has sixty days. All-in-all, you're looking at maybe a four-month timespan.

However, the Governor has the power to make a decision, at any time and once he does, you can then decide, if you want the position. If you accept it, you'll be sworn in to take over the remaining of the term left by Judge Sumner, until election time."

"For the next eight years?"

"Yes."

"And you both believe in me that much?" I ask with tears in my eyes.

"Don't you believe in you that much?" Mr. Townsend asks

"I do—"

"Then make us proud."

I get back to my office and I'm too nervous to sit. I begin pacing as tears fall from my eyes.

"God, is this your way of punishing me? Are you dangling this, in my face, only to snatch it away? There's no way, you can think I really deserve this?

Right?" I whisper. "After everything I've done, you still think I'm deserving of this? Why and why now?"

"Camille," Charles taps on the door before pushing it open.

I try to wipe the tears.

"Are you okay?" he inquires, closing the door.

"Charles, you aren't doing this because of what—"

"No, of course not," he says walking over to me. "Do you really think I'd set you up to fail?"

I cry more.

"Camille, why don't you believe in you?"

"I do but there's some things that I've done that I'm not proud of, Charles and being nominated for this seat opens my life up for the world."

"We all have a past and if we allowed our mistakes to hinder us, none of us would be where we are. Camille, the bible—"

"No bible," I state.

He takes my hands. "The bible says in Luke one and forty-five, blessed is she who believed God will fulfill His promises to her. Do you believe in God?"

"I used too but it's been a long time since Him and I have seen eye to eye."

"Then it's time you get back to Him. Camille, the God we serve, He's a forgiving God and in spite of all we do, whether good or bad, He still finds us favored. You simply need to believe."

He pulls me into a hug.

"Whatever you're toiling with, deal with it so that your fight can end." He pushes me back and looks at me. "We've all had things that leave us damage or a little broken but God works great with broken pieces. I know because I've been there."

"Thank you."

"Stop running and face what you've been hiding," he says before kissing me on the cheek and leaving.

Chapter 8

When he leaves, I sit back down at the desk, taking some tissue from the drawer. Wiping my face, I put my hands in the prayer position and close my eyes.

"Dear God, no, Heavenly Father, no; shoot!" I lay back in my chair. "Dear God, have mercy on me."

I close my eyes and allow the tears to fall because I don't know what else to say to God. I've been angry with Him, for so long, it doesn't feel right to even call on Him, now.

An instant message pops up from one of the law clerks.

Katie W: *"The Lord is good to everyone. He showers compassion on all His creation." Psalm 145:9 NTL*

"Are you kidding?" I say out loud.

Another message pops up.

Katie W: Mrs. Camille, I'm sorry. I was meaning to send that to the other Camille.

Camille S: No problem but thank you for sharing that. I needed it, more than you know.

Katie W: 😊

"Okay God," I say out loud.

I take a few minutes to get myself together. I go inside the bathroom to clean my face. Getting back to my desk, I dial Thomas' number but he doesn't answer. I decide to call my dad. It's been a while since I've talked to or seen him.

They don't even know about any of the things that have happened to me, over the last six months and I wanted to keep it that way.

I sigh, thinking about how close we used to be. I'm their only child but with them living in Miami and me in Memphis and our workloads; time always seem to get away from me.

"Judge Holden's Office, how may I help you?"

"Judge Holden please," I say grabbing a napkin and wiping my face.

"May I ask your name?"

"Camille Shannon."

"One moment please."

"Camille, is this really you?"

"Yes, daddy, it's me. How are you?"

"I'm great now that I'm hearing your voice because I thought you disappeared into thin air. Where have you been?"

"Just working, you know how it is. How is mom?"

"She's your mom, do you even have to ask," he chuckles. "Is everything ok with you? You sound like you've been crying."

"I have but it's good news. I've been nominated to fill the seat of a judge who had to step down in my district."

"Wow baby that's great but why don't you sound excited about it?"

"I just don't know daddy. I know how it was, watching you run for election and I don't know if I can handle it. People dig into every aspect of your life and right now that's the last thing Thomas and I need."

"What do you mean? Has something happened that I need to know about?"

"No daddy, it's just the usual drama that happens in any marriage."

"Are you sure because I can be on the next plane?"

I laugh, "I'm sure. This was just a shock and I need to digest it."

"Camille, if there is anybody that I know without a doubt, can handle this, it's you. You've been calling yourself Judge Camille, for as long as I can remember."

"I know but that's because I had the greatest role model, you."

"While I'm appreciative of that, you've also worked your butt off. Don't allow fear of what you think to talk you out of your position. You've been through worse and look at you."

"What do you mean?"

"Just what I said. Now, I have a case to preside over. Call me tonight because I'm sure your mom would love to hear from you."

"Yes sir."

"I love you daughter."

"I love you too, daddy."

After the call with dad, I get to work on familiarizing myself with this new case. I take off my glasses to take a break when I see the note with Chelle's name.

I open up the software on the computer when Stephanie buzzes, letting me know my new client is here.

"Send her in, please."

"Mrs. Shannon," she says walking in.

"Yes and you are Mrs. Walker, right?"

"Yes but please call me Monica and thank you for taking my case on such short notice."

"No problem," I say looking her over, "please have a seat. I've read over the submitted paper work but why don't you tell me why you're here."

"I've recently taken over my father's company, Donnington & Associates because he passed away, suddenly, thrusting me into this position. With everything going on, I want to start over fresh with a new firm to represent us. My father left a lot of things unfinished, including a merger that I'm now trying to complete."

"I'm sorry to hear about your father's passing."

"Thank you."

"This merger, is it currently being handled by another firm?"

"Yes but the old firm and I aren't seeing eye to eye on the final details. They seem to think I'm only a cute face with a thick waist because I wasn't on the frontline of his business. That's why, I want my own, representation."

"You sound like a very smart business woman."

"I wish everyone thought that because all they see is a woman in five-inch heels and a skirt and they instantly think I don't know anything."

"That's because they expect us to use what's under our skirts and not our brains," I tell her.

"Exactly. Anyway, I bought you the contract and all of the information I have on this company. I have a few weeks before I fly to Miami to meet with them. If you decide to take us on, I'd love for you to join me."

I nod as I flip through the folder of information. "This all sounds good but I'll need to meet with the other partners, first, before I can give you a definite answer. Give me today, or possibly Monday to let you know."

"Great and thank you, again, for meeting with me. I know it's a lot of information but I've heard great things about your skills in the courtroom."

"Thank you and it was nice meeting you, Mrs. Walker."

"You as well and I look forward to working with you."

"Likewise," I say as I watch her walk out.

I spend the next few hours working on the contract Mrs. Walker left. Some things weren't adding up so I ask the firm's investigator, Raul to look into them before I meet with the other partners Monday morning.

Getting ready to pack up, for the afternoon, my cell phone vibrates on the desk. I put it on speaker.

"Hey Ray."

"Hey boo, I wanted to check on you, after dinner at Shelby's, because things seem tense between you and Thomas."

"You know I'm good because I'm not thinking about Thomas raggedy ass."

She laughs. "Still, is everything ok? And don't lie either because I will be at your house before you get there."

"Yes honey, I'm fine but there is something I need to talk to y'all about but I want to talk to Thomas first."

"Something bad?" she inquires.

"No, it's actually something good, for a change."

"Great then let's meet for breakfast, Saturday. How about 9ish at the Waffle House we normally go too."

"That would be great."

"Do you want me to mention it to the others?"

"Yes, please."

"Ok, I'll see you then."

"Thanks Ray."

Again, packing up, my phone vibrates again. I pick it up to see a text from Brock.

BJ: Hey, are you free tonight?

I smile, while holding the phone.

"Hmm, am I free?" I ask myself, out loud. "I could be."

ME: Hey, not tonight but soon.

I pause before hitting send, trying to think of how I can squeeze him in. Nah, I better not. I hit send and drop the phone in my purse.

Chapter 9

Getting home, TJ is sprawled across the living room floor, doing his homework. He has his headphones in and the music is so loud, he doesn't even hear me calling his name.

Shaking my head, I walk pass the office and then the master bedroom but Thomas isn't in either which means he's either in the basement or out back. I head upstairs, into the guestroom, kicking off my heels.

"Is everything ok?" Thomas asks, walking in, causing me to jump.

"Crap," I jump. "I was looking for you."

"For?" he questions.

"What's wrong with you?"

"There's nothing wrong with me but what's wrong with you? Are you sick or something because you're hardly ever home for dinner?"

"Man, can't I do anything right? If I'm not home, you have a problem and when I am home, you still have a problem. What do you want from me because I can't continue to do this?"

"You're always the victim."

"Victim?" I chuckle. "Is that why you're sleeping with Chelle?"

"I'm not sleeping with anybody and don't start projecting your issues onto me. I'm not a cheater, like you."

"Okay Thomas."

"You ought to be grateful I'm willing to check on you, Ms. Thang."

"What is wrong with you? Did you not get the orgasm you needed, or did she bite you, while giving you head?" I ask him. "Whatever it is, I don't have time to listen to you nag?"

"Bit—"

My head snaps around.

"Finish it. I dare you to finish the last syllable and I guarantee you'll need to take some time off work."

"I'm sorry," he remarks.

"Yes, you're definitely sorry if you ever part your lips to call me a bitch, again. You know what, I'm done. I'm done trying to prove to you that I've changed and I'm done jumping through these freaking hoops, you've set."

"Hoops I've set? Sweetie, we are in the shape we're in because of you and your actions. Let us not forget that."

"How can I when it's all you bring up. Hell, let you tell it, I'm the spawn of satan, unless you're drunk and your dic—"

"That's enough. You always go too far."

"Yea, well I've gone farther than I'd planned to go, on this ride and I'm getting off."

I brush pass him and go into the bathroom, slamming the door.

Thirty minutes later, I walk into the kitchen.

"Hey," I say to Courtney, who is on her computer at the counter, "where's your brother?"

"I'm right here," he says walking in with Thomas.

"Good because there's something I need to talk to y'all about. Afterwards, we can go to dinner. First, I may be going to Miami, in a few weeks, if the firm decides to take on this new client. Since I'll be down there, I'm going to visit my parents."

"Can we go? We haven't seen them in forever?" Courtney begs. "Please."

"If you all can miss the time from school, I'll think about it. Now, before y'all get too excited, there's something else. When I got to work this morning, I had a meeting with my boss and—"

"Please don't tell me you're getting fired," Thomas says rolling his eyes.

I take a deep breath. "When I got to work this morning, I had a meeting with my boss. He informed me of my name being recommended to fill the seat of a judge, in our district, who had to step down."

"Wait, so that means you're going to be a judge?" TJ asks.

"It's possible."

"Why would he recommend you?" Thomas snipes.

"Dang dad, aren't you excited for her?" Courtney asks.

"I'd be more excited if I thought she was ready for it."

"What does that mean?" I inquire.

"With everything you've been through, over the past few months and seeing it hasn't been long since you've returned to work; I don't think you're ready for it. Besides, we need this time to figure out what we're doing."

"We're going to leave while y'all talk," Courtney says pulling TJ by the arm. "Mom, call us when you're ready to go."

"Thomas, we've had months to figure us out and it doesn't seem to be working. Yes, I've messed up but I've also done what I said I would. I can't keep trying to get you to see me, for who I am now so with or without this race, I think its time we call this what it is. Finished."

"Let me guess, you've already placed yourself in the running?" he asks, folding his arm.

"No, I haven't because I wanted to talk it over with my family first."

"Yea right," he scoffs, "and I bet you're going to tell me, you haven't told your girls either."

"I haven't because I thought I could come home and have an adult conversation with you about something that involves both of our futures."

"Having an adult conversation, takes two adults, Camille."

"You know what, fuck you. It seems like you're trying to sabotage everything I'm working towards. I came to you, FIRST, because I'd hoped an opportunity like this, would be something my husband would be excited about. I thought it would be a chance for us to start over. Yet, nothing I do is good enough for you.

Yes, I've messed up but weren't you the same man who was talking about restoration, weeks ago? Weren't you the same one talking about you loved me and wanted us again? You were the one who asked me to move back into the bedroom."

"Yea and I'm glad you didn't because that was a mistake, on my part because you aren't ready to be back in our bed."

I chuckle. "No, the mistake was believing you when you said you wanted us to start over." I turn to walk away but then I turn to face him. "What are we doing, Thomas?"

"I don't know. What are you doing, Camille?" he mockingly asks.

"I'm glad to know you think this is a joke."

"No, this isn't a joke but if you think, for a moment, I'm about to play the good husband; standing beside you as you're being sworn in as judge, think again."

"Wait, are you jealous?" I ask.

"Jealous? Hell no but I'm not about to act like we're the perfect family for photos and shit. We're far from that."

"You're right but nobody is perfect and I've never asked you to play anything. We've had our share of mistakes but stop acting like you've never messed up because you aren't the best husband, either."

"What is that supposed to mean?"

"It means, you have flaws, the same as I do. The only difference is, you've been great at hiding yours but I hope, you never have a day of unveiling."

He shrugs, "I ain't got no worries."

"Good, keep that same energy if you ever do. Kids, let's go."

Chapter 10

Breakfast with the Girls

"Hey boo," Ray says giving me a hug when I walk into Waffle House.

"Hey," I say sliding into the booth.

"Well dang that's all I get."

"I'm sorry Ray. I just have so much on my mind."

"Good morning ladies, my name is Jewel. What can I get you to drink?"

"Coffee for me please."

"Me as well."

"I'll take coffee too," Shelby says coming in. "Hey ladies, wait, what's wrong?"

"Thomas," I roll my eyes, "do I need to say more?"

Jewel comes back with our coffee and silverware. "Are you ladies ready to order?" she inquires.

"Is anybody else coming?" I question.

"No," Rays says, "it's just us."

We order our food and wait until Jewel walks away.

"What has Thomas done that has you so upset?" Shelby asks.

"Forget him, for a minute because I have some news." I exhale. "I've been recommended, by Mr. Townsend, as a candidate to fill the vacant seat of Judge Sumner, District Seven."

"Oh my God Cam that's amazing," Shelby says reaching over to give me a hug.

"Yes," Ray adds, "that is great news but I feel like there's more."

"More, as in Thomas' reaction to it. Y'all I know I've did some foolish stuff, last year but I really wasn't expecting him to act the way he did when I told him."

"What happened?"

"He seems to think I'm not ready and he said, I ain't playing no good husband; standing beside you for pictures and shit like we're the perfect family;" I explain, trying to imitate his voice.

"Really?" Shelby questions. "I'd think he'd be the first one supporting you. You've been talking about being a judge for as long as I can remember. Besides, I thought y'all were on the path to fixing things."

"I thought so too but each day, I don't know if I'm going to encounter, Thomas, my husband or Attorney Shannon, my judge and juror but what if he's right and I'm not ready? Y'all know all the things I've been through. Months ago, I was in the hospital barely hanging on and now," I sigh. "What if somebody finds out."

"So? Hell, we all have demons, we've had to fight in our past. You aren't exempt from that," Ray states.

"I know but people in the public, are far less forgiving than friends," I tell them. "Most of them don't want someone who has been damaged presiding over them."

"Camille, if you were to pull back the sheet, on most of the people in public positions; you'd find most of them damaged. Yet, it's not about the past mistakes but it's the present actions that you should be proud of."

"I agree with Ray," Shelby adds, "and yes, you have some skeletons but who doesn't. Everybody dead and alive have made mistakes, Camille. You aren't the first and you surely will not be the last."

I put my head in my hands.

"What else are you worried about?"

"What if I'm too damaged to be a great judge?"

"Camille, you've made some mistakes but damaged doesn't mean destroyed."

"What's the difference?" I ask looking at her.

"Let's say, I take a plate and drop it. Depending on how it lands, it could potentially shatter into pieces, right?"

I nod.

"Well, the shattered pieces of the plate, could be big enough for me to repair. Sure, there may be evidence of the plate being broken, at one time but as long as it does what it's been designed to do which is hold stuff, what I put on the plate can cover the flaws. However, here's the blessing, even if I can't repair the plate, there have been some beautiful things created out of shattered pieces. Baby, you may be damaged but God works with damaged every day."

"You better preach," Jewel says sitting our food in front of us as a few other people say amen.

We all laugh because we hadn't noticed she was standing there or that anyone else was listening.

"Sister, you need to listen to her," she tells me before walking off.

"Camille, yes you've been through a lot but Pastor Magnolia says, recovery then restoration."

"And if all people have to judge is your past then let them because you're one hell of an attorney and I know you will rock as a judge."

"I know but if I'm selected, the media won't care about my work because they'll be all up in my business trying to find out who the hell Camille Shannon is." I say, cutting into my chicken.

"And? She ain't that bad? That Cam bitch though, they better watch out for her." Ray says laughing.

"She ain't lying," Shelby says, biting into her chocolate chip waffle. "Seriously, Cam, you can't allow fear, of what if to hold you back. You're a great attorney and obviously your boss feels the same way, or he wouldn't have put his name on to recommend you."

"Have you talked to your dad about it?" Ray asks.

"Yeah, we've talked a little but I'm going to see them, in a few weeks."

"Well if there's anybody who can get you to do what is right, it's Daddy Holden." Shelby laughs.

"I know right," Ray says. "I can remember the Spring Breaks and summers we spent down there, once they moved back, while we were in college. Hell, he still scares me."

"I'm sure you'll make the right decision. Now, to change the subject, I'm supposed to have lunch with Derrick," Shelby tells us.

Ray and I shrug.

"That's all I get?" she asks.

"Girl, it's just lunch."

"I know but you don't think it's too soon?"

"For who? Shelby, you're the one whose husband died, not anybody else. You're the one who has to grieve and find a way to cope with your new way of life. Besides, it's just lunch." Ray tells her.

"And if it ain't," I say pointing my fork at her, "it's still your choice. All I ask, don't move too fast. Make decisions with your prayers, not your emotions."

"Look at you talking churchy."

"I don't know about that. Shoot, I've been trying to get back to knowing God but it's hard."

"No harder than being in this crazy world without a God who gives us new mercies every morning."

"Speaking of church, are y'all ready for Tamah's dedication?" Ray inquires.

"Yes but do y'all think Lyn will come?"

"I sure hope so. I've been calling and leaving her messages," I tell them.

"Me too and all we can do is hope."

We eat in silence for a few minutes.

"Okay," I say dropping my fork. "Dr. Nelson, my therapist doesn't want to see me anymore because he said he hasn't been helping me and he failed me; yada, yada," I wave my hand.

"Well, you did sleep with the man," Ray scoffs.

"I didn't make him," I shrug. "Anyway, he referred me to another therapist."

"Okay," they both say.

"It's a woman—"

"Aw, you can do therapy with a man but not a woman. Why? Are you scared she's going to call you on your shit?" Ray smirks.

"I'm not afraid of her but what can she do that he hasn't."

"Help you. You said yourself that you're scared of what the media may find, in your past, right?"

I nod.

"Then going to therapy can be a counterattack. Besides, it can't hurt. Try it. For us." Shelby says, sticking out her lip. "Please."

"I'm with Shelby," Ray adds. "I love you chick but there's a reason, you changed, all of a sudden."

"I didn't," I sigh. "I've always been like this and y'all know it. Having Courtney and TJ slowed me down but this is me."

Ray is shaking her head, while sipping her coffee. "While you were in law school, you turned into a different person, though. We thought it was your way of letting loose, from all the stress of your work load but baby, you didn't stop. True enough, you settled down but about a year ago, you started up again. Did something happen?"

"Yea, my husband stopped satisfying me."

"Is that all?"

"Yes y'all that's it and I'm so tired of having this same conversation."

"Then see what this new doctor is about because she can probably help you." Ray says grabbing her phone. "Shoot, I'm late picking Rashida up from driving school. I love y'all and Cam, give her a try."

Chapter 11

I'm sitting in the parking lot of Waffle House, after the girls drive off, thinking about what they said.

I get my phone and open the app to schedule an appointment with Dr. Scott. When that's done, I call Lyn's hotel room, in Jamaica.

"What's up trick? Look, I know you're probably out getting sand in the crevice of your bootie but I wanted to let you know, I'm thinking about you. Oh and I gave your contact number to all the girls so expect them to call. Okay bye, I love you. Call me."

*****

I walk into High Point for Tamah's dedication. I thought I was late enough to miss Bible study but I wasn't. I slide into a seat in the back as Pastor Reeves is teaching.

"God says, in that day. What day? The day He shall restore you. Restore, the action of returning something to a former owner, place, or condition. Let me explain something, because maybe you aren't understanding why I feel the need to run around this building.

We look at the situations, we must face and want to curse God. We complain about the moments things break us but how can God restore what ain't been broken? Oh, I know it doesn't feel good but when has been broken ever felt good?

Yet, brokenness leads us to recovery then restoration. And if God is dealing with you, at this very moment, it's because there's something broke; within you that needs His attention.

See, He's the manufacturer and creator who owns the parts needed to restore you back to wholeness. Stop fighting Him, stop forsaking Him, stop ignoring Him and let Him restore what He created."

My leg begins to shake as I lean forward, hanging on to her words.

"Let God repair the heart that's filled with holes from brokenness, your spirit that's filled with leaks from mess, your lungs that aren't functioning properly because you're breathing in the wrong stuff, your blood filled with toxins because you're around the wrong folk, your veins that are clogged with anger and your joints that are locked from non-movement. Beloved, you need restoration.

Are you willing to sacrifice you? Are you willing to give God you, if it means Him restoring you? Are you willing to give God all of you, if it means Him making you whole?"

I put my head in my hands to try to stop the tears.

"Please don't think for one moment, God can't bless us when we're broken. Baby, being broken in God is the blessing. Anybody willing? For my Bible tells me in Micah *7:8-11*, *"Do not rejoice over me, O my enemy. Though I fall I will rise; Though I dwell in darkness, the LORD is a light for me. I will bear the indignation of the LORD because I have sinned against*

Him, Until He pleads my case and executes justice for me.

He will bring me out to the light and I will see His

righteousness. Then my enemy will see and shame will

cover her who said to me, "Where is the LORD your God?"

My eyes will look on her; At that time, she will be trampled

down like mire of the streets. It will be a day for building

your walls. On that day will your boundary be extended."

Anybody ready to be restored?"

I cry out when I feel somebody's hand on my back. I look up to see Shelby and I cry harder.

"You've got to let it go, sister. Please."

"I'm trying but it hurts."

Shelby pulls me up and we walk toward the altar. On the way, we stop when we see Lyn. We all surround her. When she begins to cry out, I kneel beside her.

Pastor Reeves begins to pray. "Dear God, thank you for what you've allowed to happen in this place. Tonight, oh God I ask that you meet us at this altar, restoring every person who had the courage to make their way. Father, they're in need of restoration. Father, they're in need of you. Have your way. You don't need my permission to move me out of the way. Walk through this altar and restore," she cries out, beginning to speak in tongue.

When I feel her hand on my head, I stretch out my arms and she continues to pray.

"You can heal but you've got to move you out of the way. You're afraid of your past but it only has the power you give it," she says in my ear.

Chapter 12

A month later

"Yes, I'm in love with you, Camille but I don't know how to make you happy. I don't know how to measure up to everything you desire. Each time I think I'm ready to be with you, intimately again, I think about all the people you've probably slept with and I can't get pass it."

"Thomas, you are what I desire."

"Then why were you cheating?"

"Because you allow it."

"What?" he says, stopping mid fluff of the pillow.

"Thomas, for years, you've never cared about the times I come or go. It wasn't until, before the overdose that you even showed concern. Then, our sex life is boring as hell. You give me three pumps, missionary style and never care about me being satisfied. And you know I'm not satisfied because I tell you."

"That still doesn't mean I allow you to cheat."

"Yes, it does. If you don't care about me being satisfied, sexually that means you are allowing me to be satisfied elsewhere."

He's shaking his head. "That's not true."

"Let's say I cooked dinner and you came home starving but what I serve you, isn't good or it doesn't fill you up. Sure, you may pick at it and even eat some of it but a little while later, you'll find yourself in the pantry, looking for a snack. Thomas, I'm not trying to justify my mistakes but you leave me hungry and you don't care."

I snap out of my thoughts when my computer chimes with an inner office message. I reply back, shaking off that conversation with Thomas that was weeks ago. That night we made love in our bed but it didn't last. After a few weeks, Thomas was back to his old self with three pumps, in missionary style and a roll. A roll is him rolling off of me when he's done regardless if I'm satisfied or not.

That's why I needed Brock to knock the edge off and man. I smile thinking about the night I met him in the parking lot of Chicks and Cigars.

"Turn on your side." I direct before turning my back to him, twisting, onto my side and placing one leg on the dashboard. We're laying parallel, in the seat, just enough for him to enter me.

"Aw," I moan, grabbing his thigh. "Just like that."

I start to move in my chair, until someone taps on the door. "Come in," I say getting myself together.

"Mrs. Walker, do we have an appointment?" I ask, confused.

"No, we don't and I'm sorry to show up without one but your assistant isn't at her desk."

"It's okay, come in. What can I do for you?"

"I know it's been a few weeks since I've been in touch but when you're thrown into managing a company, it can be overwhelming. Anyway, I received some news from my private investigator and your guy, Raul about Brunson Manufacturing," she says handing me a folder.

"Have a seat," I tell her pointing to the chair across from me. "I had Raul to run some checks on them because of some red flags I saw in the original contract."

"You're right, there were a lot of those. For starters this company is a front for a major drug cartel in Miami. They're trying to get a legitimate company to take it over because the Feds are investigating them. I don't know how my father became connected to them but this was a bad deal, from the beginning."

"Did your old law firm not know this?" I ask, flipping through the papers.

"I'm sure they knew but didn't care because it was more money in their pocket. I had a hunch something wasn't right and this further proves my point."

"So, what's next?"

"I'll no longer need to go to Miami but I'd like to retain your firm as our lead legal counsel. Then, I want you all to do a deep dive into Donnington & Associates. Don't leave a stone unturned."

"Are you sure because this could potentially dig up some negative stuff on your dad," I state.

"I'm aware but if there are any unethical business practices going on, I'll shut the doors of Donnington and Associates without hesitation. My husband and I have worked too hard, for what we have to allow this to tear it all down. I never wanted this damn company anyway but dad left it to me in his will."

I smile at her when she's done.

"I'm sorry but I am tired of trying to justify myself to a bunch of men," she shakes her head.

"Child, I feel you on that but don't allow them to see you sweat. I'll have the paperwork started, for us to take over your legal duties and once the contract is drawn up, Stephanie will have it sent to you."

"Thank you and I apologize for taking up your time but I have to make sure this business doesn't misrepresent who we are."

"It's no problem but what do you and your husband do, if I may ask?"

"I'm an author and he's the state's prosecutor."

"Brent Walker is your husband?"

"Yes, he's the one who recommended you. He says, y'all work well together."

I smile and nod, "yes, we have occasionally. I'll have to give him a call to thank him."

"Please do. Oh, I'm having a small party to celebrate the release of my twentieth book and I'd love for you to come," she says reaching into her purse and pulling out a card.

"Twenty books, wow that's a great accomplishment. I'll definitely try to make it."

"Thank you again, Mrs. Shannon."

"No problem and I'll be in touch."

When she leaves, I lean back in my chair. "Well, I'll be damn."

I grab my desk phone and call Brent's cell phone.

"Camille Shannon, what do I owe this pleasure."

"Hmm, I'm a pleasure? Noted," I remark.

He laughs.

"Hey, I called to thank you for recommending your wife to the practice. It's kind of weird but she seems cool."

"She is and I knew, she needed a heavy hitter and that's you. You're the best woman for the job; for both of us," he laughs.

"Boy, bye." I hang up on him, laughing until my phone dings with the reminder of my appointment with Dr. Scott. I grab the phone and for a second, I think about canceling.

"Give her a try Camille," I hear Shelby's voice in my head. I lay the phone down and finish what I'm working on.

Chapter 13

"Mrs. Shannon, I was shocked to see you on my calendar this afternoon. Come in. How are you?"

I close the door and take a seat on the couch.

"I'm alive so that counts for something."

"The first time we met, we weren't properly introduced. My name is Dr. Geneva Scott and although, we're in this setting of therapy; I like to base our meetings on the foundation of God's word."

"What does that mean, exactly?"

"It means, I like to start and end in prayer and I sometimes refer to scriptures. Is that going to be a problem for you?"

"You're in charge and can do whatever you like," I tell her.

"No, that's where you're wrong. I'm not in charge, Mrs. Shannon, you are because I hope no one is forcing you to come."

"Nobody forces me to do anything," I snap. "I make my own choices and do what I want."

"Whoa," she says. "How about we start with prayer. Is that okay?"

I shrug.

"Dear God, as we come before your throne, I first thank you for another chance. Thank you, God for giving us mercy, we don't rightfully deserve. Thank you for keeping us and for what you're going to allow to transpire in this place. God, you have permission to intercede within this space to right any wrong, forgive us of any sin and heal. We're yours and you can do with us, what you will. Heal, deliver and while you're doing that, restore. Amen."

"Amen."

"Now, tell me what made you come back?"

"I told my friends I'd give it a try," I say, nonchalantly.

"So, you're still not here for you?"

"Does that matter?"

"Of course, it matters. May I call you Camille?"

I shrug.

"Camille, you can only get the help you need when you're willing to receive the help you need. Otherwise, we're just wasting each other's time." She stands and walks over and opens the door. "When you're ready to take this seriously and admit what you're running from, call me. As for now, you're taking up space that can be used for someone who actually wants the help."

"But I booked an appointment so technically this space, at least for the next," I look at my watch, "thirty-eight minutes, is mine."

She closes the door and retakes her seat.

"You're right but there's obviously a problem or you wouldn't have come. Camille, I am not your enemy and neither am I here to judge you. Dr. Nelson asked me to take over your care because he sees you fighting and he genuinely cares."

"He doesn't care. He's like any other man who gets what he needs. Let's be honest, doc because Dr. Nelson or Troy, didn't do a damn thing to help me."

"Yes, he did. He referred you to me because he could have easily allowed you to continually show up, get your fleshly needs met and not your mental."

"Look, can we get on with this? Don't you have some stupid questions to ask or scriptures to throw at me?"

"Camille, why are you so angry with God?"

"Who said I was?" I question.

"It's evident by your demeanor. See, you look together on the outside yet you are a complete mess on the inside. You want everybody to think you're this chick who has it all together but with one gush of wind, your entire life will crumble. You want to know why? Because you've built this person," she says waving her hand up and down, "with shattered pieces."

I look away as tears begin to fill my eyes.

"You're slowly dying on the inside because the person you've created is getting to big to keep hiding. It's like a woman who is hiding her pregnancy. Starting off, it isn't hard. She can throw on some baggy clothes or stand a certain way and nobody would be the wiser. However, eventually, the baggy clothes will no longer be able to hide what's not meant to keep hidden.

Camille, you walk in those five inch heels, you wear the nice suits that conform to your shape, you probably drive an expensive car, stay in the big house, work at your dream job and put up the smokescreen for your coworkers and friends but it won't last long. Eventually, the thing you're hiding will come out, whether you want it too or not."

I didn't realize that I'd wrapped my arms around myself and was rocking.

I open my mouth but the only thing that comes out is a moan.

"Let it come out."

"Oh God," I cry, "what do I do?"

"Stop hiding."

"I can't."

"Why not?" she asks.

I continue to rock.

"Why can't you stop hiding? What are you afraid of?"

"People will know and they can't know."

"Know what, Camille?"

"My secret. They can't know. They can't."

"Okay, okay," she says. "Then answer this. Who are you? Not the girl who lashes out when she's in an uncomfortable situation or the one who uses sex to keep from displaying a weakness. But who is Camille Shannon, in here?" she asks, pointing to her heart.

"I don't know who she is anymore. She was taken, from me, eighteen years ago and I've yet to find her."

"What do you mean, she was taken? Camille, what happened eighteen years ago?"

"I have to go," I state.

I grab my purse and head toward the door.

"Camille, stop hiding."

I stop at the door and turn back to her. "It's all I know how to do."

Getting to my car, I scream. I sit there for over twenty minutes, until I grab my phone.

"Hey," Brock answers, "I'm surprised to hear from you. What's up?"

"I could use some company. Where are you?"

"I'm leaving Chicks & Cigars; you want to meet me here or—"

"No, I need some physical company, the kind that requires the touching of body parts. There's a hotel, not far from the bar, get a room and text me the number. I'll be there in fifteen."

I hang up, lower the visor and take a wipe out of the console to clean my face before starting the car and pulling off.

Chapter 14

Standing outside of room 324, I knock on the door. He opens it and pulls me in.

"Are you okay?"

"Talk later," I say removing my clothes and pushing him on the bed.

"Oh, you're a feisty one. I like that but I suggest you shut the fuck up and listen."

"Hey, are you okay?" Brock asks, touching my face.

"Yea," I smile but when I bend down to kiss him—

"Isn't this what you've been wanting? Isn't this why you've been coming here for help? Well, I'm going to give you, exactly what you want."

I jump back.

"Camille, what's going on?"

I grab my clothes and run into the bathroom.

"Camille, baby, please tell me what's wrong?"

"Just go," I holler. "Just go."

"I'm not leaving you here, like this. Tell me what's going on?" he asks, twisting the knob of the door. "I'm going to come in, okay?"

"I've been waiting to sample this," he tells me, slapping me on the butt. "Relax and you might enjoy it."

When the door opens, I crouch down by the tub with my hand out.

"No, please don't do this." I scream.

"It's Brock and I'm not going to hurt you."

"Get out! Get out!"

Thirty minutes later, I hear Shelby's voice.

"Camille, it's Shelby. I'm coming in."

I'm sitting in the same place with my legs pulled up against me and my arms wrapped around them.

"Camille baby, what's wrong?"

"He hurt me," I cry, rocking back and forth.

"Who hurt you?"

I squeeze my eyes closed.

He finally thrusts into me and I cry out.

"Ah," he moans, pushing into me. "This is better than I expected. Ah, yeah."

She touches my arm and I jump.

"Who hurt you?" she asks again.

"Professor Frederick."

"Your law professor? What did he do?"

"He raped me," I cry.

"Oh, sister," she says pulling me into her and I cry out.

After some time, Shelby stands me up, wrapping a robe around me before leading me back into the room.

I climb into the bed.

"Brock, I'm so sorry," I tell him.

"You don't have to apologize to me. I only want to make sure you're okay."

"I am and thank you for calling Shelby."

"No problem but I'm going to get out of here and let y'all talk."

She locks the door behind him and comes to sit on the end of the bed, facing me.

"I saw him," I blurt.

"Who?"

"Professor Frederick. He's friends with Mr. Townsend and he was here, in Memphis, over a year ago," I clarify, "consulting on a case."

"Around the time you—"

"Started acting crazy. Yes, I know."

"Did he do or say something to you?" she questions and I shake my head.

"Nothing but the mere fact that he was here, was enough. Since then, I've been thinking about what he did and in order to cope, I become Cam."

"Why didn't you tell us?" she asks.

"Because I didn't want that look of pity," I say pointing to her face.

"This look isn't pity, it's pain from knowing you've been dealing with this since law school, by yourself. You could have told us."

"I couldn't tell anybody because then y'all would feel sorry for me and I didn't want that. Shelby, don't you understand that if I admitted this to anybody, I'd be considered weak and damaged. Admitting what happened to me would always have this stigma, of being a victim, tied to my name and I'm not a victim."

"Girl, being victimized doesn't mean you have to live your life as a victim; it means that something happened to you. Admitting that you were raped gives you the power to overcome it, not be victimized by it. As for us seeing you as weak that is never the case because you can handle anything."

"Shelby, didn't you see what happened to Lyn, after she was raped? She turned into a person we didn't recognize and who ran. We pitied her because she'd been damaged."

"We didn't pity her, we prayed for her. But you did the same thing, Camille. The only difference with you and Lyn, she ran to another country; you though, you hide in plain sight."

I look at her.

"You created Cam, the sex crazed chick with the smart mouth, who doesn't really think she's hurting anybody by having her way. You sleep around because that's something you can control when the truth is, you really aren't.

You're beautiful yet you probably see ugliness when you look in the mirror. You're strong but somewhere along the way, you started thinking, having a scar makes you look weak and it doesn't. You, being the victim of rape, doesn't change who you are, your mistakes do."

I wipe the tears from my face.

"You tried the drugs and you can continue to sleep around but none of these things will erase what happened to you. You have to stop running and deal with this. If not for you then do it for Courtney and others after you. You can't have this on your bloodline, because then your son and daughter will think, running is the way to deal with all their problems. Stop running and you give them a chance to survive."

"I don't know how."

"It starts with admitting you're hurting and need help. Then you have to be honest with those of us who love you. Camille, if you don't get control, now, you may not survive and," she stops, "I can't lose you too."

"I'm sorry, Shelby."

I begin to cry and she comes up next to me, pulling me into her.

"Does anybody else know about this?"

"No. I started to tell Dr. Scott but I ran out."

"Girl," she says pushing me. "You need to go back and let that woman help you."

I slide down under the cover and pull it up over my head.

"I'm serious. Either you go or I'm beating your ass."

"Okay," I exhale, pushing the cover down. "I will but first, I need to be honest with Thomas and my parents."

"I love you," she says.

"I love you too."

"I know but that doesn't mean we aren't going to talk about you and Brock."

I cover my face, again. "Nothing happened—this time."

"Heifer, what do you mean this time?"

"Didn't you just say, we would talk about this later?"

She pulls a pillow, from behind her and hits me with it.

"Shelby, seriously, thank you for coming tonight. I don't know what would have happened, had it been anyone other than Brock."

"I know and although I don't like that it was him, I'm glad it was but there better not be a next time."

"Yes ma'am."

"Let me pray for you and don't scrunch your nose because you need it."

"That you ain't lying about." I sit up and we hold hands.

"Dear God, thank you for being an all wise and loving God. Father, as I sit here, holding the hands of my sister who has been broken, I'm asking you, in this very moment to start the restoration process. Lord, I don't know what it looks like for her but give her strength to surrender and receive what she needs which is you.

It doesn't matter what happened to her, she needs you. It doesn't matter the thoughts, she's having, she needs you. She needs you to restructure her broken pieces and then put them back together again. God, she's been wandering too long, by herself. Hiding from a secret that is suffocating the purpose you've placed within her.

Please God, I'm crying out to you to deliver her and if you have to use me, use me. If I have to go down on my face, in prayer, I'll go. If I have to fast and cry out, in the midnight hour; for the chains to be broken; I'll do it because I need her free. I'm asking you God to do it. Not tomorrow but right now because she's been bound and in sorrow too long. Whew, thank you Jesus."

She releases my hands and gets off the bed walking in circles, clapping her hands and speaking in tongue. "Do it Jesus because she has to come out."

I watch in awe with tears streaming, as my sister, stretches her hands out, calling my name.

I stand and go to her. She pulls me into a hug and I cry into her shoulder. "Camille, you've got to come out."

"I'm ready," I sob. "I'm ready."

"Then so it shall be. Amen."

After a few minutes of her, praying in my ear, she pushes me away from her.

"Now, get your narrow ass into some clothes and go get your husband back by telling him the truth," she tells me.

Chapter 15

I make it home and Courtney and TJ are in the living room, fighting over the remote.

"Hey, HEY," I yell.

"Oh, hey ma," TJ says before hitting Courtney with a pillow and running.

"I'm going to kill him," she screeches.

"Before you do, where's your dad?"

She hunches her shoulders, "I don't know, he hasn't been home."

"Have y'all eaten?"

"Not yet."

"Let me shower and change clothes then we can go out and grab something because I don't feel like cooking."

"We don't have nothing in there anyway," Courtney states.

"Well, it looks like you should have gone grocery shopping."

"No honey that's your job."

"Oh really," I say grabbing another pillow and lunging it at her. "Go get your brother and I'll be ready in thirty."

"TJ," she yells, from where she is.

"Really Courtney?"

On the way to Humdinger's Restaurant, I stop at a red light and dial Thomas' number to see if he wants me to get him some dinner but it goes straight to voicemail.

I drop the phone in the cup holder and turn the radio up.

"I find space for what I treasure, I make time for what I want, I choose my priorities and Jesus; you're my number one. So, I will make room for you."

"Hey, can one of y'all download this song on my phone?"

"Huh," Courtney says, removing her earphones.

"Can you download this song on my phone?" I say pointing to the radio. "It's called Make Room by Jonathan Nelson."

"My habits, you can move that over. My attitude, you can move that over too. Whatever it is, you can move that over. That's not like you, you can move that over too."

"It's on there," she says, "in your iTunes app and you really need to add some music to it."

"Thanks," I roll my eyes at her and she laughs.

I pull up to the restaurant and drive around to find a parking space.

"Mom, isn't that daddy?" TJ asks, pointing towards the building.

I turn my head to the side, a little. "Humph," I mumble, opening my phone to dial his number. He looks at the phone and press decline.

I park. "Stay here," I tell them.

I can't see who he's arguing with but the conversation is so heated that neither of them hear me walk up.

"Thomas?"

When he turns, I realize its Chelle, the chick we had a threesome with.

"Cam, uh Cam," he says stuttering. "What are you doing here?"

"Uh, where is here, exactly because I was headed to get dinner. I guess I should be asking you, what are you doing here?"

"It's not what you think," he states.

"You sure because I'm thinking my husband is arguing with a chick he shouldn't be in contact with. Now, what the hell is going on?"

Neither of them says anything.

"I'm going to ask for the final time—"

"I'm pregnant," Chelle blurts.

"Congratulations but it still doesn't answer my question."

"You want to tell her?" she smirks.

"Both of you simple bastards are starting to piss me off. One of y'all need to start talking, now!"

"Fine, Chelle says the baby is mine," he puffs up.

"Wow," I smile. "Are you also the one funding her new career?"

He doesn't say anything.

"Say something, baby daddy or should I be talking to her."

"You can, I don't have a problem answering," she says, matter-of-factly.

"Cool," I step closer to her. "Is my husband giving you money to run your little escort catering business?"

"He is but I don't escort anymore. I have him and we're going to be together," she grins and points to the empty building. "This right here, is my new storefront. It's called, 'A taste of Chelle.'"

"A taste of—"

"Camille, let me explain."

"No need but boy, I didn't think you had it in you to cheat, let alone fund the hoe's business. I guess the jokes on me."

I go to walk off.

"He cheated because he needs a real woman. One who won't run the streets and treat him like a boy. He's all man and I plan to take very good care of him by keeping him happy and satisfied."

"Trick, the only thing you can keep happy is a man with a stiff penis. As for worrying, about y'all, nah, I'm good beloved but y'all be easy."

"Just like I thought," she smacks. "I told you Thomas this bitch doesn't love you. She ain't even willing to fight over you."

I turn to slap the piss out of her but Thomas grabs me.

"No, Camille, I can't let you hit her."

"Mom," TJ yells.

"Camille—" he stops and his eyes get big, "the kids are here?"

"Yes and had you answered your phone, you would have known but you were too busy, standing on the side of a busy street arguing with your born-again chef-thot."

I snatch away from him.

"Camille, please don't hit her."

"I'm not scared of her," Chelle screams. "She's just mad at the truth. Well sweetie, you should know that after you paid me to suck your husband's penis, I started doing it for free."

"Then you're the fool because you should always charge. Let me go, Thomas."

"Yea, let her go, Thomas," she mocks, "and let's see how fast it'll take you to lose that chance to become a judge."

"Wow," I laugh. "Not only do you cheat but you pillow talk too? Damn."

I turn to walk off.

"Cam, please give me a chance to explain."

Hearing him behind me, I turn so fast that he bumps into me. "I don't need you to explain anything because I've seen enough. I'm going to take our children inside to get some food and then we're going home. You need to figure out a way to explain this to the kids and then find somewhere else to go."

"Mom, what's going on? Who is that lady?" Courtney questions when I make it back to the car.

"We'll talk about it when we get home. For now, let's get some food."

Chapter 16

When we get home, the kids were still asking questions.

"Mom, tell us what's going on?"

"I don't know," I yell causing both of them to jump. I exhale. "I'm sorry. I didn't mean to yell but I don't have the answers you're looking for. You can ask your dad because it's him who needs to explain."

"I heard that lady say she was pregnant by daddy, is that true?"

"Son, I don't know," I say, frustrated. "I heard the same thing y'all did when you did."

"Man, this family is so screwed up," Courtney says stomping out the room.

TJ comes over and gives me a hug.

"Everything will be okay. I got you," he says before releasing me and leaving.

I'm standing at the kitchen sink with my hands gripping the edge, my head down and tears beginning to fall.

"Camille," Thomas says, startling me but I don't look up. "Camille, please let me explain."

"How long have you been sleeping with her?" I ask, softly.

He doesn't say anything.

"DAMN IT, HOW LONG?"

"Since you were in the hospital but it only happened a few times because I was stressed out. With everything we've been going through, I messed up."

"Wow," I state, stepping back, wiping my face and laughing. "I don't know why I'm crying. Maybe it's the embarrassment of you choosing her, the fact I knew you were cheating or because you pulled a me on me. Either way, congratulations boo and you need to explain this to the kids."

I move to walk pass him but he grabs my arm.

"Camille, I never meant for this to happen. I saw her one night when I stopped for a drink, after leaving the hospital and I was in a bad place. I was angry at you for all the things you'd done and on top of that, you almost died. I wasn't thinking straight."

"Oh, so let me get this straight. I'm the reason you went out and slept with someone else without a condom and produced a child? Yet, I can clearly remember you saying, your inability to please me wasn't grounds for my infidelity. Would you like to retract that statement, counselor?"

"I made a mistake Camille that's it."

"Nah boo, you made a baby," I tell him, snatching my arm from him.

"What do you want me to say?" he asks, flinging his arms in the air.

"Do you hear yourself? A few months ago, I was on the other side of this conversation, asking you the exact same thing. You told me to figure it out. Remember that? Well, how does it feel?"

"It hurts."

"You're damn right, it hurts. Mr. I Ain't Got No Worries. You're a judgmental, pompous asshole who can stand in my face reading off my sins, telling me what I'm doing wrong, every freaking chance you get yet you're no better than me. You walk around like your shit don't stank, acting like you're a saint, whose heart I broke and in a few months your mistake will be born. At least I had the decency to use condoms."

"It may not be my baby."

"There's a possibility it is, though." I shake my head and laugh, "You've done a great job at pretending with your, I'm in love with you, Camille but I don't know how to make you happy. I don't know how to measure up to everything you desire because I can't get pass you cheating," I mock using a deep voice, "bullshit!"

"I'm sorry but what did you expect, after years of putting up with your shit, huh? You've taken advantage of me, as your husband and now that you're wearing the shoes of hurt, you see just how heavy they are. Well newsflash sweetie, we're in this situation because of you. You were the one who bought Chelle into our lives. You were the one who never appreciated what you had. You did all of this, not me." He yells.

"Yeah, you're right. You're absolutely right. I've made a whole lot of mistakes because I'm not perfect but nothing I've ever done has been bought to our doorstep."

"That doesn't make it right, Camille."

"I DIDN'T SAY IT DID," I yell. "Thomas, for as long as we've been together, I have always made sure, you were satisfied sexually—"

"It's always about sex with you," he cuts me off.

"Let me guess, it wasn't about sex with Chelle? A known prostitute who I paid to service you, for your birthday? Then what is it? She must have been the one who talked you out of quitting law school, every freaking week because you said it was too hard? No? Then was she the one who worked two jobs so you could focus on passing the bar exam, the second time because you flunked the first one?

No? Then, was she the one who cheered for you with every case you won, big or small; washed your clothes, took care of your house, held you while you cried over the death of your mom, took care of your children and prayed for you.

No, no; she was the one you struggled with, the one who was there when we couldn't even afford to pay rent and had to eat Vienna sausages because you were too proud to ask my parents for help. Tell me, Saint Thomas, was she the one because clearly cheating with her, isn't about sex."

"She, she," he stutters, "she—"

"She, she, she what?"

"She acted like she needed me," he confesses.

"She stroked your ego? Did she call you big daddy, while she ran your bath water or put on your bib, for you to eat so you wouldn't mess up your clothes, too?"

"You know what I mean," he states. "It wasn't all about sex. Look Camille," he moves toward me.

"No," I say putting up my hand, "because here's the truth of my situation. Cheating hasn't been about sex for me either. And after the day I've had, I came home to be honest with you but you weren't here. All you've ever heard was that I was unsatisfied with sex and while I am, it was so much more. See, you not caring about me, fed into the low self-esteem created after—"

"After what?" he questions, cutting me off, again. "You really expect me to believe you have low self-esteem? Girl bye."

"No, I don't expect you to believe anything. Good night, Thomas."

"Go ahead and walk away, like you always do."

"I walk away because you never hear me. You only hear what you want. Yes, I've made mistakes and I'm sorry for everything I've done but I tried being honest about what I needed. You, though, you act like you're perfect.

Here, I thought, in the far corner of my mind that your criticizing and questioning my every move was because you really cared. Truth is, you just wanted to make sure we didn't cross paths. Well, good job because you sure had me fooled."

Chapter 17

A couple of days later, I'm meeting Judge Alton, for coffee to discuss my decision to move forward with the nomination.

Pulling up at Republic Coffee, I get out when I see him standing outside.

"Hey," he says giving me a hug. "You okay?"

"Yeah, I didn't sleep well last night but nothing that a strong cup of coffee can't help."

"You know, the coffee may help you, temporarily but dealing with what's keeping you up, will help you sleep."

"All this time I thought you were a judge but I had no idea you were a preacher too."

"Come on," he laughs pulling my arm.

Stepping inside, I hear someone call my name.

"Lyn, where has your ass been?" I ask throwing my arms around her. "I haven't seen you since Tamah's dedication."

"I know," she smiles. "I've been a little busy."

"Lyn this is Judge Charles Alton and Charles this is Lyn, one of my best friends."

They exchange pleasantries and I ask him to get me a blueberry muffin and a white chocolate mocha. When he walks off, I grab her by the hand.

"Slut, what is it?"

"What are you talking about?"

"You know what I'm talking about. What has put this smile back on your face?"

"I hope it's me," Paul says walking up behind her.

"Oh shit, hey brother," I say hugging him. "So, y'all been sneaking around acting like teenagers?"

Paul hunches his shoulders.

"No but we've been figuring things out. We don't know what those things are yet but when I know, I'll tell you."

"Okay then. Well, I'm not going to hold y'all but we need to talk when I get back from seeing my parents in Miami."

"Of course and Ray told me about the recommendation, congratulations."

"Thanks and Lyn, I'm happy that you're happy, again."

"I'm getting there."

She kisses me on the cheek. "I love you sister."

"I love you too and Paul, take care of her."

"I will."

Before I can make it to where Charles is, my cell phone rings with a number from the police department. I sit my purse on the table.

"This is Camille Shannon."

"Mrs. Shannon this is detective Craig Harris from the Memphis Police Department. I hope I didn't catch you at a bad time."

"Detective Harris, no but what can I do for you?"

"Your name has come up, in a report, filed by a young lady who says she was assaulted by you."

"What," I laugh, "are you serious?"

"Yes and I'm only calling because we've worked a few cases together and I wanted to get your side of the story. Can you come and speak to me?"

"Yeah, I'll be there in 30 minutes."

"What was that about?" Charles asks, looking at me with concern.

"According to Detective Harris, a young lady filed a report saying I assaulted her."

"What lady?"

"The only one I can think of is the chick Thomas has been seeing."

"Did you?"

"Hell no but now I wish I had."

"I'm going with you."

*****

"Mrs. Shannon, it's good to see you again," Detective Harris says, holding out his hand.

I take it, standing up. "Harris this is my friend and attorney Charles Alton."

"You didn't have to bring an attorney because you are not under arrest."

"I know but I'd rather be safe than sorry."

"No problem. Follow me," he says leading us into an interrogation room.

"I'm not going to hold you long but a young lady showed up at the precinct, claiming to have been physically assaulted by you."

"Can I see that?"

He hands me the piece of paper.

"Wow," I laugh reading Chelle's statement.

"How do you know, Ms. Michelle Craft?"

"I met her when I hired her to do a threesome with me and my husband for his birthday, a while ago."

His mouth opens. "Uh, have you had any contact with her since then?"

"Not sexually but she recently catered a Valentine's Day dinner at my friend's house. Apparently that's her new business that my husband is financing but I didn't assault this trick. Detective, the only thing that saved me from slapping the taste out of her mouth, is time and the fact that my children were there."

"Time?"

"Yes, as in, I don't have time to be risking my reputation over a trick whose profession is laying on her back. I have too much to lose and if anything is going to mess up my record, it surely won't be an ass whooping."

"Look, Mrs. Shannon, I don't know what's going on in your personal life but anyone who will go through with knowingly filling a false police report is crazy, I suggest you watch yourself."

"Will there be any charges filed?"

"Not against you, because I got the surveillance tapes right before you got here and found out, Ms.

Craft is a liar. Since you were already on the way, I wanted to give you a heads up. We will be charging her for filing a false report."

"No," I tell him. "As much as I'd like that, I believe, filing that report will only make matters worse. Can we just let this go?"

"Honestly, Mrs. Shannon, it's not up to you but I will speak to the District Attorney's office."

"Thank you, Detective. Please let me know if there is anything else, I can do."

When we make it to the parking lot, I am fuming.

"I've got to be dreaming. This can't be happening," I say pacing. "Please tell me all of this is a nightmare."

"It will be alright but you have to calm down."

"Charles, I don't think the time is right for my name to be in the running for this nomination."

"I do."

"Why, after everything that's going on?"

"Camille, I've watched you grow as an attorney over the years. You face criticism from men, who were threatened by your strengths and it only made you hold your head up higher and fight harder. I've seen you tear down walls and not be bothered by the rumors of sleeping your way to the top. Baby, this nomination is exactly what you deserve."

I exhale. "Thank you for coming with me."

"Anytime," he says. "You know I have your back."

"I'll see you later."

Chapter 18

Getting inside my car, I dial Thomas' number.

"You know, it's one thing to find out about your affair and love child but to have your baby momma try to ruin my reputation; is crossing the line." I state before he can say hello.

"What are you talking about?"

"Being interrogated by the Memphis Police Department, for a report filed by Michelle Craft, saying I assaulted her. Do you know how embarrassing this shit is?"

"She filed charges? Camille, I didn't know but why didn't you call me?"

"I'm calling your ass now. Look Thomas, this girl could ruin my life and my career and for what? You? Hell, she can have you but when it comes to my name and reputation, she's crossing the line. And know this, the next time she comes for me, recommendation or not; I'm kicking her ass."

I hang up and throw the phone into the passenger seat.

*****

"Good afternoon Camille."

"Good afternoon, Mr. Townsend. Please, come in and have a seat."

"I wanted to check in with you. I know being blindsided by the vacancy of Judge Sumner's seat, was a lot to take in but I really do think this is a great opportunity."

"I, as well and that's why I turned in the questionnaire but there's something we need to talk about."

"Okay," he replies, looking worried.

"I'm going through some things, in my personal life. Things that will be handled but I don't know how my marriage will look, once everything is settled.

With that being said, there's a young lady who tried to file a police report against me, for assault."

"Assault—"

"I didn't assault anyone," I interrupt. "I went to the police station this morning and there's evidence that I did nothing to her so there'll be no charges and I asked them to not file anything against her, for the false report."

"Do you know who the lady is?" he questions with concern.

"Yea, my husband's mistress."

"Wow," he says sitting back in the chair and loosening his tie.

"I know this is a lot to process and if you need to pull my name out of the pool, I'll understand."

"Camille, I will not lie and act like this isn't some heavy news. It is, because being a family woman, can go a long way in you being confirmed for this position. However, you are a strong woman, whether you're married or not and I still believe you're the best for this.

All I ask, is that you be open and honest with me. In the meantime, I'm going to contact the firm's publicist and give her a heads up. That's if you're still wanting to be included."

"I do but the backlash of my personal life, in the media, is my only concern."

"That's why I pay for the best publicist, on this side of the Mississippi. She'll handle the media, while you keep doing what you do best and that's practice law."

"Yes sir and thank you, again for believing in me."

"No thanks needed. All I want you to do is make us proud."

"I'm going to do my very best." I tell him. "Have you heard anything from the Judicial Committee?"

"Not yet but as I stated before this can take upwards of four months. We should be hearing, the Committee's three nominees, any time now. After that, it's in the Governor's hands."

"And after his selection, the person is sworn in as the replacement?"

"Yep and although it seems like an easy process, it isn't because your background will be looked into to ensure you're the right person for the job. It doesn't get as ugly as the actual election but it's still a public position. You have to be ready for whatever is thrown your way because the person chosen, will fill this chair for the next eight years."

"Wow."

"Camille don't overthink this, worrying about the future. Take it one step at a time," he tells me, reaching over and placing his hand on top of mine. "You're already prepared for this. I've watched you these last ten years and you've worked hard for this and if I didn't think you were ready, I never would have put you in the position."

"Mr. Townsend, I'm not worried about doing the job but my biggest fear is being picked apart by the media if I am chosen."

"Again, that's why we pay a publicist. You take some time to visit that old fart of a father and tell him he still owes me a bottle of scotch."

"Yes, sir and thank you Mr. Townsend."

He pats my hand and then leaves. A little while time later, Stephanie buzzes to say that Lyn is here.

"Hey Lyn," I say coming from behind my desk. "Is something wrong?"

"No, nothing is wrong. Am I interrupting you, because I can always come back?"

"Girl get in here. You want some coffee or water?"

She shakes her head.

I motion for her to sit and I join her on the couch.

"Now, tell me what's wrong because I know you. You were all smiles this morning but now, it looks like you got the weight of the world on your shoulders."

"Am I wrong for wanting to try again with Paul?"

"Hell no. You and Paul have been together since Kermit and Ms. Piggy, shit. If anybody deserves a second chance, it's y'all."

"I know but I'm worried about Kandis because the whole baby momma thing is a whole other beast to tame. Do you know she lied about being pregnant? Paul said, it was a lie. Girl, I don't know if I could have dealt with her being pregnant again."

"Don't I know," I say exhaling.

"Cam—wait, what do you mean?" Lyn asks, confused.

"Chelle is pregnant by Thomas."

"Girl stop lying. Old square head ass Thomas cheated? Nah, I don't believe it. Hold on, Chelle, isn't she the one—"

"We had the threesome with, yep."

"Damn," she says.

"Yea, I had to congratulate this mane, for pulling a me on me because truth is, I can't be mad. This is me getting back what I've put out."

"Sister, what are we going to do?" she asks laying her head on my shoulder.

"I don't know but I can't go on like this. Once I get back from Miami, he and I are going to sit down to decide. As for you, if you want your husband, get your husband."

"I'm just scared of failing again because I don't know if I can take any more shots to the heart, Cam."

I raise her up. "Lyn, you're stronger than you give yourself credit for. You've survived things that would have killed the average person and look at you. You're smiling again and I hope you're finally sleeping."

"It's getting better," she says as Stephanie buzzes.

"I'm going to get out of here but call me when you get back from Miami," she says giving me a hug.

"I will because there's something I need to talk to y'all about."

She stops and looks at me.

"I'm good," I reassure her.

"Okay. I love you."

"I love you too."

Chapter 19

Stephanie buzzes again.

"Yes ma'am," I say pressing the intercom button.

"Camille, Mrs. Walker is on line one for you."

"Thanks Stephanie." I sit at the desk and press the speaker. "Mrs. Walker, how can I help you?"

"Mrs. Shannon, I was calling to see if you've turned up anything on my company? I have a meeting with the board on next week and they keep asking why I fired our other legal firm. I am so sick of going toe to toe with these assholes, I could scream," she says letting out a breath.

I laugh.

"I apologize. I didn't mean to say all of that but since I've taken over, I've been getting is flak from the men who thought another man should be the head."

"You don't have to apologize. I totally get your frustration. I am actually meeting with my investigator, later today and I'll give you a call afterwards but look, don't allow those men to see you sweat. You can vent to me but in front of them, keep it together. They are waiting for you to have a woman moment because to them that makes you weak. You got this."

"Thanks Mrs. Shannon."

"Please call me Camille and you're welcome," I tell her.

"Oh, I sent you an email about the location and date change for my party, did you receive it?"

"Yes and I'll be there."

"Great and thanks again. I look forward to hearing from you."

Later on, towards the end of the day, Raul comes in.

"Hey Camille, I finished the investigation on Donnington & Associates and everything checked out. All of the audits have cleared from a financial point of view and so did back ground checks."

"That's interesting. Mr. Donnington seemed to have had all of his stuff in order, huh?"

"Yes, he did. The only thing that wasn't legitimate was the other law firm they had. I'm not sure why Mr. Donnington was in business with them because they were charging him an extremely high rate. On top of that, they knew this company in Miami would have sunk them had they purchased it."

"That makes me wonder why Mr. Donnington would even use this law firm, in the first place. He had to know they had shady practices."

"He could have, or they were really good at covering it up," he remarks.

"You're right. I'm glad Mrs. Walker followed her instinct and had them investigated before finalizing that merger. Thank you, Raul. Can you please email me, all of this information and Mrs. Walker?"

"You're welcome and I've already sent it. Is there anything else you need from me?"

"As a matter of fact, there is. I need you to look into someone, for me but off the record."

"Sure. "

I write Chelle's name down on a piece of paper.

"Who is Michelle Craft?"

"She's the woman who claims to be pregnant by my husband. Find out everything you can on her. I'm headed to Miami, on Friday and I'll be gone a week but you can reach me on my cellphone with anything you find."

"Will do and have a safe trip."

On my way home, I decide to stop by Chicks & Cigars. I go inside the Humidor room and get a cigar before stopping by the bar.

"Hey, you good?" Paige asks.

"Yes and look, I want to apologize—"

"No need, I shouldn't have pushed my fetishes off on you without first asking if they were okay. I'm sorry and maybe, you'll give me a chance to make it up to you."

"Maybe," I smile.

"Are you drinking your usual?"

"Yea."

"I'll take care of it and bring it to you, along with everything else. Find a seat."

I go over to a corner and sit. A few minutes later, Paige comes over with my Hennessey and Ginger Ale, a cutter and torch. She hands me the glass and takes the cigar from my hand.

I watch her cut it, before rolling it in her mouth to moisten the end and lighting it. Before handing it to me, she kisses me.

I smile.

"Let me know if you need anything."

An hour later, security comes in to let me know someone threw a rock through my window.

"Are you freaking kidding," I say getting up.

Once outside, I turn the alarm off and open the driver's door to see a rock with a note in the seat.

"Wow," I laugh.

"Camille, are you okay?" Paige asks coming up behind me.

"Yea."

"I'm going to call the police," the security guard says.

"No, it's okay. I don't need that kind of drama."

"Are you sure?" he questions and I nod.

"What does the note say?"

I hand it to Paige and she reads it out loud. "Karma is a bitch, bitch. Damn babe, who have you pissed off?"

"Who knows."

"Camille," I hear someone call my name.

"Brock, hey."

"What's going on?" he asks, rushing up to me.

"Someone threw a rock through my window," I shrug.

"Are you okay?"

"Yes, I'm peachy." I turn to Paige and the security guy. "Do y'all have cameras?"

"Yea but it'll take a few days to get the video," she tells me.

"And I can tell you that it was a guy, in a hoodie. I didn't get a good look at him because I thought it was his car, until I heard glass shattering. I tried to stop him but he ran off."

"Figures," I tell them, reaching into the door to get some paper towels to clean the glass from the seat.

"Do you need me to call somebody, for you?" Brock asks, looking at me with concern.

"I'm good, I promise. I'll drive home and get this fixed, tomorrow."

"At least, let me follow you home," Brock request.

"You—"

"Please, it'll make me feel better."

"Sure."

He goes over to speak to the guys he was with while I thank Paige and security, giving them my card to send any camera footage. When I see Brock's car, I drive off. Twenty minutes later, I pull into the garage and wave at him before lowering it.

Chapter 20

I go inside to see Thomas in the den, asleep on the couch. I kick his foot, harder than I had too.

"Ouch," he sits up. "What's wrong with you?'

"Your bitch that's what."

"What are you talking about?" he sighs.

"First, she files bogus charges—"

"She said she didn't."

"Oh, right because she wouldn't lie."

"I am only telling you what she told me," he states.

"I guess she's going to tell you she didn't have someone bust the window out my car tonight, either?"

"Someone bust your window? Where?" he stands and comes over to me.

"Doesn't matter. I'll have the surveillance footage soon and then I'm pressing charges, on her."

"Where we you and were you in the car?" he asks again.

"What difference does it make where I was?" I ask him.

"You must have been somewhere you had no business. That figures."

"Somewhere I had no business? Who dictates what business I have and where it should be handled, Thomas?"

"Me, your husband."

"Oh, I get it," I laugh. "You think I was out cheating."

"Were you?"

I turn and walk upstairs. He follows me into the guestroom and closes the door.

"Get out."

"Not until you tell me where you were."

"I don't have to tell you nothing. You lost the ability to question me when you got your girlfriend pregnant."

"She's not my girlfriend but how do you know it was her, who bust your window? It could be anybody."

"Anybody other than your precious baby momma, who you keep taking up for."

"I'm not taking up for her but you can't go around accusing people."

"Why not? Hell, you do it to me, all the time."

"I'm sick of having this same argument with you."

"And I'm sick of assuming you want this marriage," I tell him.

"I do want this marriage, why else would I still be here?"

"To annoy me," I shrug then laugh. "Maybe this is karma for everything I've done to you or it's God's way of punishing me for breaking my vows. Either way, I can't keep doing this. When I get back from Miami, I'm going to find somewhere else to stay and file for divorce. Now, get out," I say walking over to open the door.

He grabs my arm, turning me to face him and closes the door. "I'm not going anywhere and you're going to listen to me, for once."

"I don't—"

"Damn it, Camille." The sound of his voice causes me to jump.

"I'm sorry for yelling but I've put up with so much of your shit and never once did I say divorce. The nights, no the mornings you'd come in from doing God knows what, I was right here. When you threw in my face, your cheating, I still gave you chance after chance. The night you overdosed—"

"Don't."

"No," he says pushing me back against the wall. "The night you overdosed, I gave you the option to stay and get help but you left and we all know how that worked out. You, laying in the hospital for seven days and I was right there, watching you fight for your life."

"Yea when you weren't with Chelle."

"This isn't about Chelle," his voice bellows. "What happened between us, has been over for a month and I can't go back and erase that but right now, I'm talking about us. Camille, I've always been here, for you, even when I should have put your ass out and now, the first time I mess up, you want to leave me. Well, you can't because you owe me more than that."

I snatch my arm away from him.

"I don't owe you anything."

"Like hell! You owe me the same freaking thing I keep giving you and that's a chance. Camille, I made a huge mistake but why is my sin costing more than all the ones you've committed? Why should I have to pay with our marriage when you almost paid with your life and yet, I'm right here? Am I not worth, fighting for?"

I slide down to the floor.

"You don't get to decide that we're over. You have to fight for me, at least once because I deserve it and damn it, you're going to do it."

"What's the point?" I ask, feeling defeated. "All we do is fight and it isn't good for us or our children. This isn't love, Thomas and all we're doing is setting them up to go through the same thing and I can't keep doing this fighting with no resolution."

"Then let's find a resolution. Camille, sometimes fighting is good, if you're fighting because you care and for the right stuff. Look," he states, sitting in front of me, "somewhere along the way, we allowed our connection to short out. Instead of keeping the spark, between us, we've allowed space and time to blow it out.

Now, we're two people, sharing a space, instead of two people sharing a spirit and if we're going to survive, we have to reignite the connection. Yes, we've both made mistakes, we've both done and said stuff that we shouldn't have but we can't end, not like this."

"I hear you but Thomas, how are we supposed to get reconnected when you don't trust me? Hell, I can't even go out without you thinking I'm cheating."

"That's because you keep giving me reasons not to. I asked you where you were, tonight and you wouldn't answer."

"Because I'm tired of being treated like a child."

"Then start acting like an adult," he states.

I look at him.

"I said what I said," he asserts. "Your problem, you don't like it when someone challenges you. You're good at being in control and when you aren't, you lash out. Well, I'm tired of it. You will not walk all over me, anymore. Either we're going to be two adults, trying to fix this marriage or we're not.

Shit, I should have given up on you, a long time ago but I haven't because there's still some good in there," he says pointing to my chest. "and if there's a chance of finding the Camille Shannon, I fell in love with, I'm willing. And you owe me a chance of not giving up on me."

He pulls me into his lap, as tears fall from my eyes. I wrap my hands around his neck and cry.

"Squeeze tighter," he orders and I do. "I love you Camille, even with every flaw you have, because you're mine. If you weren't, I wouldn't be here, fighting for us."

"You have a baby—"

"No, there's a possibility and if the baby is mine then we'll reconvene and figure out the what's next. For now, you aren't letting me go and I'm not letting you run. I'm going to start listening to you and you need to do the same.

He wraps his arms around me, squeezing me harder.

"This tightness that you're feeling, is what my heart felt like as I watched you in that hospital bed. There were nights, I sat beside you, praying God would give us another chance. He did, Camille and although we've made mistakes, they can be forgiven."

I cry into his shoulder.

"I forgive you," he whispers, "for everything. Will you forgive me and give me and us another chance?"

"Yes," I whisper.

We stay, in the middle of the floor, wrapped together, for a few minutes. He begins to rub my back and I move against him, moaning when I feel his body responding. He kisses my neck.

"As much as I want to make love to you, I can't because it'll only complicate what we've yet to resolve."

I release him and stand up. He gets up.

"Are you mad?"

"No, I'm horny and after all that, I need my husband."

"I know and I need my wife but I need all of you, Camille and not just pieces. Don't allow, my not right now to overshadow everything we just discussed. Please."

I turn to walk into the bathroom but I stop.

"I was at the cigar bar."

"What?" he inquires.

"Tonight when my window was shattered, I was at the cigar bar, by myself."

"Why was that hard to admit?"

"Control," I shrug. "As long as you thought, I was cheating, I controlled your emotions and the situation."

"Babe, I'm your husband, not someone you have to compete with and that means, not trying to control everything. The same way, you ask me to trust you, you have to trust me enough to know I want what's best for you. You're my wife and when you aren't well, neither am I."

I roll my eyes. "You're right."

"What? Did, did you, Camille Holden Shannon just admit that I'm right? Oh, Elizabeth, I'm coming—"

"Forget you."

He laughs before pulling me into a hug.

"Babe, we have to give us another try. It's going to be hard but I got to believe that it's also going to be worth it."

Chapter 21

Miami

"Syl, they're here," I hear my mother yell as we're getting out of the car.

"Grandma," the kids scream, running to her.

"My babies, I've missed y'all so much," she says with tears in her eyes.

"Mom, don't cry," I tell her, walking into her arms after she releases the kids.

"I'm so happy to have you here. I've missed you, Camille." She pulls back and looks at me. "Have you been sleeping?"

I roll my eyes.

"Where's daddy?"

"Here I am," my dad, Sylvester Holden sings, walking down the steps.

I let mom go and run into his arms.

"My baby girl," he says squeezing me. "I've missed you."

. "I'm sorry for not visiting more."

"Do better," my mom says grabbing Courtney's arm and going into the house.

"Where are your bags?" dad laughs.

"They're in the trunk, let me help you."

"No, I got it. Go on inside. Your mom has lunch prepared."

I walk in and look at the house, like it's the first time I've seen it.

"If you visited your parents more, you'd know about the renovations."

"I know and I will but the changes you all made are beautiful."

She loops her arm into mine. "Thanks and for the record, I'm happy you are home but I miss you."

"I miss you too."

"Your dad told me your name has been entered to fill an empty seat in your district. I don't know why you couldn't call and tell me yourself but whatever, I'm still proud of you."

"Thanks but I haven't even been nominated yet."

"Girl, you are the best woman for the job. Why are you doubting it?"

"I don't know mom, it's a big decision."

"Yes and it's one that I know you've been working hard for."

"I have but being chosen, means I have to open my life to be scrutinized by the media."

"Listen, don't let the fear of that stop you from claiming this position. Yes, the media can be relentless but so what. Everybody has a past and if we allow fear—"

"My daughter is afraid of something?" dad asks coming into the kitchen.

I let out a deep breath.

"What is Thomas saying?"

I roll my eyes.

"Camille?"

"Thomas and I are in a bad place, right now."

"What did that motherfucker do?"

"Sylvester!"

"What Sylvia? I'm asking a valid question."

"It's not just him because I have faults too. We've both been unfaithful," I clarify.

"All baby girl, you can get through that," dad says waving his hand.

"Yea but he has a baby on the way and it's with a girl, I allowed into our bed."

"Aw hell no," they both say together.

"Shit, I need a drink," dad shakes his head, walking out the room.

"I'll fix it because we all need one," I reply, walking over to the bar. "You still drink crown and coke?"

"Yea but this calls for a double shot of bourbon. Now, let me get this straight. You invited a woman into your bed and now she's pregnant, by Thomas."

I nod.

"Did it happen the night, all of you were together?"

"No, they've been seeing each other."

"Is this why you're afraid of the possible nomination? You think this will get out?"

"It's not just that. It's the fact of being in the public's eye, period. Dad, I've done some things I'm not proud of."

"Camille, you're already in the public's eye. Every time you step foot inside a courtroom, you're in the public eye. You were the first woman who made partner, at your firm which means, you've been in the public's eye so, what aren't you telling us?" Mom questions.

I sit down on the couch, as she sits on the edge of dad's chair.

"Where are the kids?" I ask her.

"They're in the basement. What is it?"

I take a deep breath. "Almost a year ago, I overdosed."

"What," mom exclaims, "and you didn't tell us?"

"I never wanted you to know. I was stupid, irresponsible and mad at Thomas. I stormed out of the house and ended up in a hotel room. Some girl gave me some drugs and I took too much."

"Camille," my dad says with a tone that lets me know, he's disappointed.

"I know you're disappointed, in me but not more than I am, in myself. I'm sorry," I tell him.

"Lil girl let me tell you something," mom says standing, "hold your head up. There is no human being living or dead, who is or was perfect. Hell, we all make mistakes but don't allow your personal life to stop you from the purpose God has placed on your life. This is your destiny and if it's ordained, no man can stop it."

"I feel like such a failure though."

"The only thing you failed at is keeping this crap a secret from us. Camille, we're your parents and no matter how old you get, we're here for you." Dad barks. "You seemed to have forgotten that. We're your parents and we should have known you were sick."

"I know but—"

"There is no but," he yells. "You don't keep stuff like this from us."

Mom touches his arm and he exhale.

"I'm sorry for yelling, Camille but you're our only daughter. It's bad enough that your miles away but if something happened—" he chokes up, "you don't do that. You don't get to pick and choose what you share with us."

"I'm so sorry," I cry.

"Are you better now?" mom questions.

"Yes," I reply, wiping my face, "and I'm sorry for not telling you but I couldn't bear, letting you down."

"Daughter, your dad and I aren't perfect, by a long shot and we stay in the public's eye. Your dad's first election was hard but becoming a judge was something he's always wanted. I knew that before we got married so I prepared myself for it. Will there be some hard stuff to deal with? Yes but that comes with wanting more. If everything you desired was easy, what would you fight for?" mom states.

"Listen baby girl, becoming a judge and staying a judge is hard but if it's something you want, you work your ass off to do it. You're one hell of an attorney because you've placed your mark in a field that has been male dominated for as long as it's been around. However, you've got to stop letting fear beat you at the game you set the rules for and stop making stupid ass mistakes." Dad adds.

"And yes," mom says, "the media will pick your life apart, hanging onto everything you do but each time they run with something negative, give them something positive. However, you can't do that when you're off your game. Get your shit together."

"I should come home more often."

"Yes, you should. Now, get up and give your momma a hug before I go and pray this mess off you."

I stand and she hugs me, tightly.

"I'm sorry."

"Stop apologizing, for the same thing. Learn from it and don't make the same mistake again."

"Yes ma'am."

"Have you been going to church?"

"Not like I should."

She releases me and steps back.

"That's your problem, you done messed around and forgot God. How many times have I told you—"

"Keep God first," we both say together. "I know ma."

"You know but you're mad at Him when God ain't done nothing to you. That's alright, I'm taking you to see Pastor Moreland before you leave."

"He's still alive?"

"Yes, bite your tongue," she says popping me on the lips. "I'm going to have him lay hands on you because I don't know what has gotten into you."

"Ma—"

"Go and wash your hands so we can eat because I invited some family over later."

"Why tonight?" I ask pouting.

"Because it's my house and I make the rules."

I look back at my dad and he's sipping his drink.

"Dad?"

"You heard her. Hell, I got to sleep with her, after you're gone and you ain't cutting off my sugar."

"Ugh," I say, leaving out the room.

Chapter 22

I'm laying across the bed, in the room I used to sleep in when I was smaller. This house is the one my grandparents built, back in the 50's and where my mom grew up. Mom and Dad were both born in Florida but we moved to Memphis when I was eight or nine with dad's new job at a law firm.

Once I left for college, they moved back. I visit, sometimes but the last few years, coming home has been far less. Looking back, I realize staying away is my way of not having to deal with everything.

Being around my parents, always feel like I'm being interrogated and they can spot a lie, a mile away. If they ever found out what happened to me, in law school, they'd flip.

"Camille are you ready?" mom yells for the 50th time, pulling me out of my thoughts. "Family will be here soon and you're still up there primping."

"I'm coming."

"Mom, why is grandma freaking out about this party?" Courtney ask coming into my room.

"She's just excited about us being here that's all."

"Dang, then we've definitely got to start coming here more often."

"Alright lil girl, watch your mouth and let's go before your grandma comes up here swinging."

Walking into the kitchen, I stop when I see her talking to a chef.

"Um, Mrs. Holden, I thought this was going to be a small get together," I remark when she's done.

"It is."

"Then why did you bring in a chef?"

"Who Jules? Girl, he's been our chef for the last three years. You would know that if you came home more often."

"Okay, I get it. I need to visit more."

"Yes, you do. Oh, before I forget, one of my clients is having a book signing tomorrow night and you're going with me."

"Which client?"

"His name is Johnie Jay and he's an author, from Detroit. His third book released two weeks ago and it's already slated to be featured in Essence."

"When did you start representing authors?"

"Um, I'm an entertainment lawyer, remember? And—"

"If I came home more often, I'd know." I finish her sentence with an eye roll then I hear my Aunt Sara's voice. "Auntie," I run to her, throwing my arms around her.

"There's my baby. Look at you, looking like you looking," she says spinning me around. "Memphis has been good to you I see. All that southern cooking is going right to this ass and hips."

"I know and it looks good doesn't it?" I laugh giving her another hug.

"Only you would think so," my cousin Teresa, Aunt Sara's daughter, mocks, walking in.

"Hey to you too, Reese," I reply, rolling my eyes.

"Oh, hush up because your skinny ass could use ten more pounds," her mom states.

"Ten pounds, are you crazy? I'll never be bigger than a size four," she says with her nose in the air, as this fine cream color dude walks up next to her.

"Yes, we all know which is why you've yet to give me a baby," he states putting an arm around her waist. "Hey, I'm Noah, Reese's husband. You must be her cousin Camille, the attorney?"

"I'm just Cam but yes I am. It's nice to meet you."

"Likewise. Would you mind, later, if I can ask you some questions about the bar exam."

"Sure. Are you studying to take it or just getting prepared?"

"I'm scheduled to take it in two months."

"Congratulations. I'd be happy to answer any questions you have."

"I'd bet you are," Reese says under her breath.

"Did you say something Reese?" I step back and ask.

"Well if it isn't Camille Holden."

I turn to see who's calling my maiden name. I have to stop myself from laughing when I see the face and body of my old summer boyfriend, "James?"

"Girl, stop acting like you don't know who I am."

"With all of this," I say rubbing his stomach, "I almost didn't recognize you."

"That's what eating good does for you but I see you haven't aged a bit."

"And we see you need glasses," Reese says before walking out the room.

"It's good to see you, James," I say while looking in Reese's direction. "What have you been up too?" I ask walking to the door, leading out to the back patio with him behind me.

"From where I'm standing, it looks like I should have been up to Memphis. Damn girl you're fine."

"Ok, down boy because I'm sure you are married."

"Yea but what's that got to do with anything? She ain't here and I know you haven't forgotten how I use to lay this pipe down."

"Boy please, we were teenagers and you sure weren't laying pipe, back then. Maybe it was a tube with the air seeping out but definitely not pipe. Besides, a lot has changed since then."

"It sure has and if you let me take you around the back of this house, I'll show you."

"Uh, I'll pass but thanks for coming."

Fat pervert!

"Did you say something?" Noah ask startling me.

"Oh my God, you scared the crap out of me."

"I'm sorry. I heard you say something so I thought you were talking to me."

"No, I was talking about James and I didn't realize I'd said it out loud," I say laughing. "Do you want a drink?"

"Sure, what are you having?"

"A glass of wine."

"I'd take a beer."

"I'll be right back." Walking over to the bar to get our drinks, I couldn't help but wonder what in the hell Noah saw in my cousin Reese. Don't get me wrong, she's a gorgeous woman but she's also a whiny brat.

We're six months apart, in age and used to be really close growing up but she's always been jealous of the relationship with my parents. I've never understood the hatred she has for me and I don't spend a moment harping on it. She was the one with the problem not me.

Chapter 23

"Here you are," I hand the beer to Noah.

"Thanks. Now Camille—"

"Call me Cam. No one calls me Camille but my parents."

"Ok Cam, how have you liked being an attorney?"

"I absolutely love it. However, I'm a little bias because it's all I've ever known, seeing that both of my parents are attorneys. For as long as I can remember it's what I knew I wanted to do. What about you? What made you decide to go into law?"

"I guess you can say my desire to help people because that's all I've ever known," he replies. "My mom is a teacher and my dad's a police officer. Growing up, I watch them be dedicated to their jobs and they have a heart of giving. I want to work in the community."

"And Reese is going for that?"

"Of course. She knows how passionate I am about my work. It's my calling and that's why I wanted to ask you about the bar exam. I heard it can be brutal."

"It can be but that's why you have to be prepared. Create a study schedule and stick to it. Buy some quality study materials, none of that cheap stuff because the cheap always comes out expensive. More than anything, ask questions and practice. I can't tell you the many hours Thomas and I spent, getting prepared. There would be days, I didn't leave the house but it's so worth it."

"I know it will because I love everything about the law and helping people. I only hope I am as good as you and your parents."

"I'm only as good as the effort I put in and I make sure to be a hundred percent, in every case that's attached to my name."

"Thanks," he says.

"No problem but back to Tight Teresa. I never pegged her as the type to want to do any kind of community anything. When she became a teacher, it shocked the hell out of me."

"Why?" he asks sipping his beer.

"I don't know, it's just her whole vibe that I can't see standing in front of a classroom, let alone being nice to kids." I shrug. "Anyway, how did y'all meet?"

"She's not as bad as you think," he tells me, "and believe it or not, she loves teaching."

"I'll take your word for it."

He laughs. "I met Teresa through our best friends. We dated for about a year and I knew she was my wife."

"Aw, how sweet but you can be honest with me. How is it being married to her? Is she always this dry and snobby?" I question, sipping my wine.

"She's definitely a brat, for sure but underneath her tough exterior, is a very lovable person."

"You sure? I could have sworn that girl was made of metal."

He laughs, again.

"What's so funny?" Reese ask when she walks up and we both stop.

"Nothing, I was telling Noah an old law joke."

"Yea okay," she says rolling her eyes. "Where's your husband Cam? Don't tell me he has finally wised up and divorced you."

"Yea, we've been divorced now for three years."

"Really?" Noah asks. "I'm sorry."

"Nah, I'm lying. My husband is at home. He's working on a big case and couldn't get away. Reese, you should really lighten up because life couldn't be that bad."

"Fuck you, Cam."

"If only you weren't my cousin," I say winking at her and standing, "because an orgasm will probably do your ass some good."

"Why are you laughing with her?" I hear her ask Noah but I keep walking, out towards the pool. I sit in one of the chairs when my phone rings from a restricted number. I hit decline but it rings again.

"This is Camille Shannon."

"Mrs. Shannon, my name is Lauren with Channel 2 News. Did I catch you at a bad time?"

"That depends on the nature of this call. What can I do for you Lauren?"

"There's been talk of your name being in the race to fill Judge Sumner's seat in District 7. Would you be willing to confirm or deny?"

"I have no comment."

"Is it true that you may be going through a divorce?"

"What? Where did you hear that?"

"I can't reveal my source but is it also true that your husband, um, Attorney Thomas Shannon has a baby on the way with his mistress?"

"What did you say your name was again?"

"Lauren from Channel 2 News and if you are willing to give me the exclusive on your nomination, I won't run this story."

"Well, Lauren from Channel 2 News, you may run whatever story you have but you may want to fact check your source."

I hang up and throw the phone down.

After mingling with family and friends for way longer than I wanted too, I go in search of my mother. One of my cousins said they went out the back door.

I hear them giggling. "Mom, I'm going to call it a night," I tell her when I finally find her and my aunt Sara, behind my dad's shed. "Wait, is that a joint?"

"Girl, hush and brang your narrow ass over here," Sara says, pulling me around the shed.

"Sylvia Holden, I know you're not back here smoking weed?"

"I sho am," she says passing it to me. "Here, it may do you some good."

I hesitate.

"Girl, here, hell."

"I'm just in shock," I say before taking a pull from it. "Whoa, this is good."

"I know," my aunt smiles. "I get it from this little boy down the street. It's called wedding cake and if you smoke enough, it'll have you hornier than a girl on her wedding night."

We all laugh.

"Sylvia?"

"Oh crap," mom says pulling a small bottle of spray from her bosom. She sprays so much that we all start coughing.

When dad walks up, we straighten up.

"Woman, I know you are not out here corrupting my child," he says. "Give it here."

She takes it from behind her back and hands it to him.

"I can't believe y'all would be out here smoking," he pauses, "without me." He pulls from it and closes his eyes. "Whoa, this is good," he says looking at the joint.

"Wait," I laugh, looking from him to my mom, "you know what, I'm going to bed. Goodnight and I'll see y'all in the morning."

I hear them laughing as I leave.

I stop by the bar for another glass of wine on the way to my room to take a hot shower. I get to my room, undress and step in under the hot water. I didn't realize how tired I was until this very moment.

I step out of the shower and oil my body with the body butter, from The Bubble Bistro. Slipping on a gown and grabbing my glass, I walk out of the bathroom to turn the cover down just as there is a knock on the door.

"Mom, you in there?"

"Hey TJ, what's wrong?"

"Nothing. Grandma said you'd gone to bed so I wanted to check on you. Are you okay?"

"That's sweet baby but yes, I'm good, just tired. How are you?"

"I'm good."

I reach out my arms and he come over and gives me a hug.

"Thank you for checking on me but go on back downstairs and enjoy the party."

"Okay. Goodnight and I love you."

"I love you too."

Chapter 24

By the time I finally get in bed, I see a text notification, from Thomas. I pull the cover up and grab my headphones before reading it.

Thomas: Hey. Just checking on you and the kids. Text or call to let me know you all are okay. I love you Camille.

Instead of replying, I Facetime him.

"Hey," he answers yawning, "I wasn't expecting you to call."

"Why? Are you busy?"

"No, it's just not customary for us to talk, lately, especially on Facetime. Are you okay?"

"I'm good but I got a strange call from a reporter. First, she asked me about the nomination but then she wanted to confirm if you and I were getting a divorce because of the baby, you have on the way."

He pops up. "Are you serious?"

I sigh. "Thomas, I'm tired and I don't know what we're doing."

"Do you love me?"

"Love doesn't—"

"Do you love me, Camille?" he asks again.

"Yes, I love you Thomas but so much has happened. Honestly, I don't know why you still want me, after everything I've put you through this last year and a half."

"I don't either," he laughs and I give him a funny look.

"Don't get hung up on," I smile.

He finally stops laughing and we both get quiet.

"I don't know the last time I've seen you smile."

"To be honest, I haven't had a reason too because things have been crazy and nonstop. Now, you throw in the recommendation for judge and, I don't know."

"Camille, we aren't the first couple to go through stuff like this and we won't be the last. Sure, we're in a complicated situation, right now but the day I married you, I vowed to love you until death, in good and bad. Haven't we allowed enough stuff to break our vows?"

"Yea," I yawn, "too much for the average person."

"Good thing, we aren't average. Babe, we've experienced a lot of good, over the years and we didn't give up. All I'm asking for now, is a chance to see if we can make it through the bad. Will we make it? I hope so but if not then we can say, we tried. Can you do this, for me? Will you be willing to try, for me?"

I open my mouth but all that comes out is a whimper.

"I didn't mean to make you cry but I love you Camille. If I didn't, I would've been gone but you're my rib. Your mistakes caused some damage to the rib and although it's underneath the skin, unseen, it can still dish out pain, especially when you take a deep breath. My mistake is the bruise that shows on top of the skin. Sure, the bruise is a result of the damage to the rib but if you heal the damaged rib, the bruise will go away. We can heal, from damage but not destroyed. Without a rib, stuff can penetrate organs, like the heart and we can't have that. Babe, we have to heal."

"I don't know how," I whisper.

He sits up and turns on a light.

"I was in the guestroom, tonight and I saw the paper laying on the nightstand that looks like bible study notes. You know how long it's been since I've been to church and I almost walked away without reading them but when I started, I couldn't stop.

Psalm thirty-four, verse seventeen, says, *the Lord hears His people when they call to Him for help. He rescues them from all their troubles.* You may not know how to get healing but it's right here. Bible says, God will hear us, if we call on Him."

I'm full on crying, by now.

"Camille?"

"I'm here," I sniff.

"We have to get through this. I don't know what it's going to take, what we have to give or even the things we have to lose; but if we both put forth an effort, it has to work, right?"

I sniff.

"Can we make a pact to try? Listen, folk run to God when they're in trouble, I get that but I don't know what else to do. So, I say, we call on Him. We start by praying for each other. It doesn't have to be face to face or out loud but every day, we pray for each other. Will you?"

"I will."

We both get quiet for a few minutes.

"When did you become so spiritual?" I ask.

"I'm not but we can't keep going like we have been and if that means, becoming spiritual; I'm willing. Besides, I've been talking to Michael, whose been going to church with Kerri and I promised him, I'd visit. Camille, we've worked too hard and put too much into each other to give up without a fight. If you can't do it for you then do it for me. Fight for me, this time."

"Thank you," I tell him.

"For what?"

"For not giving up on me. After all I've done and said, you're still willing to give me another chance. I don't understand it and maybe it isn't for me too but in the meantime, will you forgive me?"

"I forgive you. Will you forgive me? I know, the mistake I made with Chelle, is huge—"

"I forgive you."

"I'm not crazy to think all our troubles are over, by having a few conversations but we have to start somewhere, right."

"I," yawn, "agree."

"I'm going to let you go so you can get some rest. If I know your mom, she probably has a full week of activities planned."

I laugh. "You're right."

"Goodnight Camille, I love you."

"I love you too and," yawn, "and I'll call you in the morning."

I hang up the call and go to iTunes to play the song I had Courtney download.

When the music begins to play, I close my eyes.

"I find space for what I treasure and I make time for what I want. I choose my priorities and Jesus, you're my number one."

The tears start again as I begin to pray, out loud.

"Dear God, forgive me. Please forgive me, God. I am so sorry for everything I've done. I've been outside of your will, too long, thinking I didn't need you. I'm so sorry. I need you, more than I realize and now I'm asking you to come into my life.

You have my permission to move anything and anybody who can hinder me getting back to you. And God, I don't know what you have for my marriage but forgive me, for taking my husband for granted and if it's your will, put us back together. Amen."

Chapter 25

I roll over and the music, from last night is still playing. I turn it off and plug my phone and earphones up to charge.

Before getting out of bed, I remember the conversation with Thomas so I sit on the side and take a few deep breaths.

"God, I thank you for another day of being in my right mind. I thank you that no hurt, harm or danger fell on me and my family. Now God, I know I haven't served or prayed, as I should but will you forgive me. Forgive me of all sins and work on me. While you're working, please touch my husband. God, I don't know the plans you have for us but whatever your will is, do it.

All I ask is for strength, wisdom, knowledge and courage to face what I may not understand. I'm not perfect but I believe you can still use me. I've messed up, enough, already and I'm tired. I need you to take over. Right any wrongs and make any crooked place straight. Set the order of my day and bear with me," I chuckle, "because I'm not the easiest to get along with but don't give up on me. Thank you, God and amen."

*****

"Good morning baby girl."

"Hey daddy," I say walking over to give him a kiss. "Where's mom and the kids?"

"They went to help her with that party thing she is doing tonight."

"Oh dang, the book signing. I need to go and find something to wear because I hadn't planned on going out."

"Yea, because you know once your mom says something, there is no going back," he laughs. "I'm just glad you're here so I don't have to go."

"Oh, so I'm your get out of jail free card?"

"Yep, thank God."

"What do you have planned for today?"

"I'm heading to play golf with a few law fellows. Why, do you have something planned because I can cancel if you want to hang with big daddy."

"Big—you know what, no big daddy, we have plenty of time to hang out. I'll do a little shopping but call me when you get done and maybe we can meet for lunch."

"Sounds good. Enjoy your day."

"Thanks, big daddy. Love you."

"Love you too."

I hate shopping because it works my nerves. Usually, I'd go to Lyn's store and let her style me but since I'm here, I have to do it myself and it's driving me crazy. I'm in the fourth shop after visiting three in the last two hours with nothing. *Ugh!*

"Are you ok?"

I look around, stunned because I hadn't realized I sighed so loud.

"Yea, I'm sorry. I just don't like to shop." I say turning to face the young lady. "Sam? Samantha King?"

"Camille Holden? Oh my God. What has it been, 15 years since I've seen you?" she asks, giving me a hug.

"Give or take but you look great."

"You too. How have you been?"

"I've been great, can't complain. What about you?"

"Good, great actually. I'm married now with two children and I own two boutiques, here in the city, for over ten years now."

"That's awesome."

"Thank you. Now, are you looking for anything, in particular?"

"Something for a party my mom is dragging me to tonight. I think it's a book release so nothing too fancy."

"Cool, follow me and I'm sure I can find you something. You're a size twelve?"

"Yes. You have a good eye."

She smiles before leading me back to a dressing room.

"Is there anything you wouldn't wear?"

"Nope," I tell her.

"Great, then make yourself comfortable. Can I get you something to drink? Wine, coffee or water."

"Some wine would be great."

I kick off my shoes and sit on one of the ottomans and wait. A few minutes later, she taps on the door.

"Okay, I have a few outfits, I think you'll like," she says handing me a glass of wine before hanging the clothes, on the hooks.

Watching her, I'm pleasantly surprised at the selections because they're all my style. Taking a sip of the wine, I sit the glass down and stand.

"This one, is a new arrival," she stays grabbing a tangerine colored, dress with one sleeve. "It'll pair nicely with the stiletto sling backs, I just got in. I also have these black, dressy shorts that will pair great with this top. It has an opening, starting at mid back and will flow over. Either of these will be good for you."

I start to remove my shirt and then my shorts.

"Let me try the dress."

She turns and stops. "Uh, you won't need a bra with this one."

Instinctively, I unfasten the bra and drop it on top of my clothes. I hold out my hand, for the dress but she's standing there.

"I'm sorry. I didn't mean to make you uncomfortable," I say covering my breasts.

"No, you're good. My apologies for staring but you're gorgeous."

"Thanks."

I take the dress and step into it. Turning to face the mirror, she comes behind me to fix it. Her hand runs over my shoulder, down my arm and then she smooths the dress down.

"Uh, I like this but I think I'm going to try the shorts and top," I tell her stepping away. "Do you have shoes to go with this outfit."

"Yeah, I'll get them."

When she leaves, I slide the shorts on, just to be sure they fit and I quickly get out of them, putting my shorts back on. I can't take the chance of something happening, in this dressing room.

By the time she comes back, I'm sitting on the ottoman, fully dressed. She comes over, standing in between my legs with my head right at her breasts.

"Size seven and a half, right?"

"Yea, thanks."

She hands me the shoes but doesn't move. Instead, she rubs her hands over my face before raising my head. Right when her lips get close to mine, my phone rings.

I exhale and close my eyes, "I need to get that."

She steps back and I grab my purse, getting my phone. I clear my throat and answer, while she grabs the clothes and shoes and walk out.

"Hey dad. No, I'm about to check out now. Garcia's? Okay, I'll be there in thirty."

Hanging up, I lean forward and sigh. "Lord, Jesus, don't allow me to fall into temptation."

Chapter 26

After meeting, my parents and the kids for lunch, I'm in need of a nap and time to relax until I have to get dressed for this party, mom is dragging me too. As soon as I lay across the bed, my phone vibrates with a text from Thomas.

THOMAS: Hey, I hope your day is going great. Love you.

I send him a quick text before I close my eyes.

"Mom," I wake up to Courtney standing over me.

"Hey, what's up?"

"Grandma sent me to wake you up. She said the car will be here in two hours to pick y'all up."

I reach over on the nightstand and see that I've been asleep for over three hours.

"Dad called. He wants you to call him."

"Okay. Where is TJ?"

"He went with Aunt Sara."

"Oh Lord, there's no telling what she has him into," I say shaking my head. "What are you going to do tonight?"

"Granddad is taking me to the movies," she beams.

"You're up, finally. How do you get anything done, sleeping midday?"

"Mom, please no lectures. I'm up and will be ready by the time the car gets here."

"Good. You know I don't like to be late."

When they both leave, I fall back on the bed.

I get my phone and dial Thomas' number but he doesn't answer. I wait a few minutes before getting up to shower. Once I'm done, I lay out my clothes before I do my makeup.

Dang girl! I say to myself when I'm done. I put on some matte lipstick, grab my clutch bag and shoes, heading for the door.

"Wow mom, you look great!" Courtney says when I come down the stairs.

"Thanks boo. Where is your grandmother? I thought she'd be at the door screaming my name by now."

"She's in her office, on the phone."

"Tell her I'll be in the den," I say as my phone vibrates.

"Hey," I say to Thomas, putting the phone on speaker and walking into the den. I lay it on the arm of the couch, while I put on my shoes.

"Hey, sorry I didn't answer earlier. Got caught up in this case," he sighs. "What are you up too?"

"You know, I don't think we've talked this much, over the phone, in the past year."

He laughs. "That's sad, right?"

"Definitely," I reply. "I'm getting ready to go with mom to a party for one of her clients. Are you still at work?"

"No, I'm actually about to meet Mike, Todd, Anthony and Brock at this new cigar bar."

"Chicks and Cigars," we say at the same time.

"You know it?" he inquires.

"Yea, I've been a few times. That's where I was when my window was broken. As a matter of fact, if Paige is working the bar, ask her about the surveillance video."

"I will but I didn't know you liked cigars?"

"Yea, occasionally," I answer. "Maybe it's something we can do together."

"I'd liked that," he says getting quiet. "Anyway, I was just checking in with you. I see the fellows walking up."

"Okay babe, enjoy your night."

I finish putting on my shoes when I hear a woman's voice. I grab the phone and realize he didn't hang up so, I press mute.

"Thomas?"

"Chelle, what are you doing here?" I hear him ask.

"I followed you. Why haven't you been answering my calls and texts?"

"Look, I told you to email me any information relating to the pregnancy and I'll be there. Other than that, we have nothing more to discuss. Now, excuse me."

"You weren't saying that, a week ago when you were occupying the space between my thighs," she says.

"Take your hands off me and for the last time, leave me and my family alone."

"Your family," she laughs. "Man, fuck your wife."

"Look Chelle, for the final time to leave my family alone."

"Or what?

"Or you'll regret it."

"Like last time?" she purrs to him, "Because the last time, you punished me, I didn't regret a thing. When you're angry, you fuc—"

"Camille," I hear my mom call out. "The car is here."

I quickly hang up and dab my eyes, trying not to smear my makeup before standing.

*****

"Mom, this is great. You do this for all your clients?"

"Yes, if they are worth it."

"How is that determined?" I question.

"By their ability to work hard for themselves. When they show me, they believe in themselves, I have no choice but to work hard for them and you'll see that Johnie Jay is one hard worker."

"What book is this for him, again?"

"This is his third and I got word, before we left the house that it has made the New York Times Best Sellers list."

"Wow that's amazing. What does he write?"

"Erotica."

"Erotica? You represent an erotica author?"

"Yes, what's wrong with that? Sex sells Camille. Come and let me introduce you to him."

"Momma, please don't tell me he is an old white man with a big belly and beard," I say following behind her.

"Oh child, he is far from that but you'll see for yourself," she smirks.

"There's my magic potion," a fine specimen of a man says before grabbing my mom up in a bear hug, leaving me standing with my mouth open.

He has dreads, hanging pass his shoulders that look like he pumps, daily, in the gym. His biceps are glistening, in his short-sleeved shirt, showing tattoos that make you wonder if his sweat is sweet.

Mom's laughter brings me out of my daydream. "Johnie, this is my daughter Camille and Camille, this is my bestselling author Johnie."

"Camille," he says letting my name roll off his tongue, as he looks me over from head to toe, "it's nice to meet you."

"Johnie, please call me Cam and it's nice to meet you as well." I say extending my hand while licking my lips.

"Cam, I see you've inherited good looks from your mom because you are as sexy as she is," he smiles, slowly rubbing his thumb over my hand.

"You're quite the charmer. I see why this place is filled with women."

"What can I say, they love my big ego," he smiles.

"Yea, I bet that's what it is."

"Okay, let's get this party started," mom says clearing her throat.

"Cam, promise me you won't leave until we've had a chance to finish this conversation."

"I wouldn't think of it. I'm going to find the bar." I say walking off to leave them to whatever business they had.

After a few drinks and mingling throughout the party, I finally settle in a corner to watch my mom, work the room. To see her, in her element, has me in awe. I know she's an awesome business woman but it's been years since I've actually seen her in action and although were at a party, it's no different.

She's working the room like it's a courtroom and she has trained Johnie Jay well because he is just as good. *Yes, I've been watching him too.*

I swing around on the bar stool and catch Johnie looking at me so I decide to give him a show. I spread my legs slowly and run my hand up my thigh. I didn't have to go far before he loses his train of thought with the group of people he is speaking too.

I turn around and smile.

"Something sure has you smiling."

"I'm sorry, I didn't hear you," I say to a random dude who interrupts my thoughts.

"I'm trying to see what made you smile like that and what I can do to continue it."

"I was wondering if Johnie Jay taste as good as he looks," I say sipping my drink while random dude walks off.

Chapter 27

When he leaves, I turn around and start to replay the conversation, between Thomas and Chelle.

You weren't saying that, a week ago when you were occupying the space between my thighs.

"Can I buy you another drink?" another random dude asks.

"It's an open bar," I say with a bit of an attitude.

"Can I get you another drink, then? Hi, my name is Anthony."

"Cam and no thanks, I'm good."

"You are definitely that because you're one gorgeous black woman."

"Thank you, Anthony but what brings you to a book signing, for a male author who writes erotica?" I question, looking at him.

"I lost a bet with my sister but she said I'd be able to meet some beautiful women and she was right. What about you?"

"My mother is the attorney for the author."

"Your mom supports this dude?" he asks, looking grossed out.

"Is there a reason she shouldn't?"

"The way my sister talks about this dude and his books, all he writes about is sex." He says, moving closer to me.

"That's what erotica is and there's nothing wrong with it. Don't you like sex?"

"Yeah but I don't need another man telling me how to please my girl."

"Oh, is his books guides to better sex?" I inquire, confused by this entire conversation.

"No but I still don't need advice from him."

"Then why are you bothered? Unless, you're actually threatened by him and not his writing."

"Mane, I ain't threatened by that sucker. I know how to please a woman."

"Okay."

He grabs my hand and puts it between his legs. Smiling, he begins to move it around. "Girl, I don't have no issues pleasing a woman. I'll have you calling your momma."

"Yea, to pick me the hell up. Have a great night, Anthony." I tell him, grabbing my purse from the bar while the bartender laughs.

"Mom where is the restroom in this place?"

"There's a public one, right outside the doors or you can use the one, in the back, meant for VIPs," she says pointing me in the direction.

I go out to the one, in the hall but it's full so I head to the other one. When I'm done, I wash my hands and fix my hair before opening the door to.

I'm startled to see Johnie, walking into the office.

"I thought you were leaving without finishing our conversation," he says walking me back into the restroom.

"Why would I do that when I said I wouldn't?"

"You are one sexy woman, Camille."

I stop when my legs hit the sink.

"Do I have your permission to touch you, Camille?"

"That depends on what you plan on touching and what you'll use."

He smiles. "I'm only going to use my hand and I plan on touching the very essence of you that God created."

"God created everything on me. Be more specific, Johnie."

"I'm going to touch the part of you that has the power to make a man weep."

"My mouth?"

He laughs. "Your other set of lips."

"Aw, then yes sir, you have my permission to touch."

He unbuckles my shorts, letting them drop before admiring my panties. He slides them down, before lifting my leg.

I lean into the sink as his hand roams. I moan, gripping his shoulders. He growls, in my ear.

He stops when we hear the door to the office open and someone knocks on the door.

"I'm, shi—I'm coming," I reply to whoever it is.

He smiles, before stepping back and bending down to get my shorts. He hands them to me but keeps my panties.

"Meet me tonight," he requests, shoving my panties into his pocket before washing his hands.

"I'll think about it," I tell him, grabbing some paper towels to clean myself up before putting my shorts on and washing my hands.

"You will," he replies with certainty, handing me an envelope with his hotel key card and room number and opening the door.

"And where have you been?" my mother questions when she sees me.

"To the restroom mother."

"And it just happened that Johnie disappeared at the same time."

"Really? I haven't seen him but I have to go. I left someone waiting at the bar."

I walk off before she can say anything else because she knew I was lying.

"Hey," Anthony says when I get to the bar. "I want to apologize for earlier because I was out of line."

"It's cool. I know you were trying to prove you're a manly man and all but this is 2019 that shit don't work for real women."

"Damn, just kick a brother while he's down."

"I'm not trying to be harsh but I'm trying to stop you from embarrassing yourself again."

This time, he grabs and kiss me.

"Ni—boy, what the hell is wrong with you?" I say pushing him away and grabbing a napkin.

"I'm trying to show you how good I can be to both sets of your lips," he smiles, big.

"Kissing like a toddler? Dude, I don't know who pumped you up to think you're God's gift to women but you aren't. First of all, your cologne stinks, your penis can't be felt through jeans and what you call kissing is too freaking wet. Nobody wants your saliva on them, especially not me and the next time you pull a stunt like that, I'm beating yo ass."

"I'm sorry," he says.

"Anthony, I don't know the type of women you've been dealing with before but either you make a lot of money or they are naïve as hell. A woman wants you to take your time when you're making her feel good. When you are kissing her lips, whichever set you choose, it's all about her. Make her remember you in her dreams when you're done. Learn a woman's body before you think you know how to please it."

"Are you telling me that you know a man's body well enough to please him?"

I exhale, leaning closer and lowering my voice. "It's all about knowing what men want. See, I can take my tongue and start from your ear, make a trail down your neck, stopping to pay extra attention to your nipples because some of y'all like them to be sucked.

Then I'll move down to your belly button and linger there just for a moment, rubbing my chin against the stubble you have on your stomach. Then, I'll make my way down to the package, I've been waiting to unwrap," I lick the tip of my finger and moan. "I'll take him into my hands, rubbing up and down before sliding him across my lips. Slowly, I'll—"

"Ok, stop," he says leaning away from me.

"Damn," the bartender says.

"Come back to my place," Anthony begs.

"No thanks love," I reply giving off the bar stool.

Chapter 28

I leave the bar, trying to find mom because I'm ready to get out of here. When I don't see her, I step out into the hall and pull my phone from my purse.

It's been off so I turn it back on to see a text from Thomas.

HIM: I hope you're enjoying the party.

ME: Almost as much as I enjoyed listening to your conversation with Chelle.

"Hey, you okay?" mom asks, scaring me.

"Hey, I'm good. You?"

"Yes, we're wrapping up so, give me a few minutes to grab my things and we can head out."

"I'll be right here."

When she walks off, I look at the hotel key card as my phone rings with a call from Thomas.

I decline, flipping the card over in my hand. He calls again. I decline, again.

"You ready?"

"Yep," I say dropping the card in the garbage.

Getting home, I walk into the den, kicking off my shoes.

"Camille, are you sure, you're okay? You were really quiet on the ride home."

"I'm tired."

"You want me to fix you some warm milk or something to help you sleep?"

"No mom, I'm mentally and emotionally tired," I sigh, sitting on the couch.

"Baby, what aren't you telling me? What's wrong?"

I start to cry then I get angry for crying. "For the last year, I've done a lot of things I'm not proud of. From cheating to the overdose."

I hear her exhale.

"For as long as I can remember, I've wanted to follow in your and dad's footsteps. Not that you all made me but because I admired y'all so much. You're strong and bold, never looking like you've had to endure anything. And I feel like a failure, sometimes because of the mistakes, I keep choosing to make. That's why I don't come home because if you knew; you'd be so disappointed in me."

"Baby girl, you haven't disappointed us."

I look up at daddy, who I didn't know had come in.

"Dad—"

"Camille, we've all done things we aren't proud of and maybe we messed up by not allowing you to see our struggle. However, life for us haven't been all roses either. We've done and said things, you wouldn't be proud of but you make amends, learn from them and don't try to make them again." Dad tells me.

"I've made so many," I whisper.

"Girl suck this shit up," mom says. "What you're going through now this is called life. Hell, it ain't easy."

"Sylvia," my dad bellows.

"No Sylvester," she says standing up, "we've babied her too long. Camille, you know right from wrong. Okay, you overdosed but you're alive. You cheated, who hasn't? What are you going to do about it, now? You can sit here, wallowing in misery or you can get your ass up and do something. Get a therapist. God knows, I love mine."

"You're in therapy?"

"Yes and have been for years. Look Camille, sometimes the pressure of this life can be heavy and if you don't know or learn how to balance it, it'll smother you. Don't be too proud to ask for help and don't dish out shit you can't take."

My mouth is open and I look at daddy.

"Don't look at your daddy. I've had this same conversation with him. You're just like his black ass and although I love y'all, it can be too much, sometimes."

"Wait—"

"Shut up Syl because you know it's true. Little girl, your daddy was a hoe, just like you are and it took him almost losing me to realize what he had. I'm willing to bet, the only reason you're crying now is because Thomas pulled a you, on you. Deal with it. Either woman up and fight for your husband or leave him alone. And you're going to church in the morning. Goodnight."

Dad and I are left looking at each other.

"She's right," he says hunching his shoulders and walking out.

Getting upstairs, I remove my clothes and makeup then take a shower. When I'm done, I get into bed with my phone.

I scroll through the texts and missed calls from Thomas before putting it on the charger and laying down.

The only reason you're crying now is because Thomas pulled a you, on you. Deal with it. Either woman up and fight for your husband or leave him alone.

I pick the phone up and call Thomas.

"Camille, baby, please let me explain," he says as soon as he answers.

"Thomas, stop. I don't want to keep living like this. I know I've made a lot of mistakes and pushed you away. Everything you've done, lately, you have every right to do because I haven't treated you like my husband. I broke our vows—"

I stop as a sob escapes my lips.

"I need help," I cry. "I need—"

"I'm coming," he says before hanging up.

I grip the phone on my chest and cry. "Jesus, I need your help. Please deliver me."

Chapter 29

The next morning, I walk into Wayside Baptist Church. Momma made me sit down front with her since the kids went to youth church and daddy is a deacon.

Mom touches my leg.

"Stop fidgeting."

After a hymn, devotion, congregational song, altar call and a song from the choir; Pastor Moreland gets up.

"That's not Pastor Moreland," I whisper to mom.

"Yes, it is, Pastor Moreland, Jr., his son and don't get any ideas because I'll knock you out."

"Ma—"

"Shh," she mouths and I roll my eyes.

"Good morning Wayside, God is good."

"All the time," the congregation says in response.

"This morning church, have you ever found yourself in a car with more people than it actually held or been in the middle of some mess that made you feel uncomfortable? In other words, have you ever been in an uncomfortable place?

In Genesis 37, we encounter Joseph, seventeen years old, the eleventh son of Jacob and firstborn of Rachel who is despised by his brothers. You know the story, don't you? Joseph is thrown into a pit by his brothers because they were plain ole sick of him and his mess.

Sure, he was anointed but he was also an instigator. Sure, he was strong and capable of being who God needed but he was also a troublemaker. He was the kind of person who could dish out stuff but went running to daddy when he couldn't take it.

His brothers were fed up and came up with a plan to throw Joseph in a water pit then lie to their daddy like an animal ate him. Now, Joseph finds himself in an uncomfortable place, partly for his actions but also because his brothers were plain tired. Anybody ever got to a place where you keep giving folk chance after chance and they keep hurting you?

Maybe you've never gone as far as Joseph's brothers but being tired can cause folk to walk away from a marriage, after twenty years. Being tired can cause people to call quits on something they've worked hard for. Being tired can have you plotting the death of somebody you love.

Yet, there's hope. Hope to get you out of your uncomfortable place. See, although we fail God with our actions, He doesn't fail us. No, he doesn't because even after all of our mistakes, shortcomings and flaws; God still loves us and He's already prepared an escape plan. It's called praise.

In Genesis, it only mentions the name of two brothers during this story. Rueben whose name means, He has seen my misery and Judah, whose name means thanksgiving or praise. See, it was Rueben's idea to put Joseph in the cistern and Judah's idea to bring him out so that he might be sold.

Rueben's name means misery and Judah's name means praise. In other words, it was misery who put Joseph in the uncomfortable place and it would be praise that'll pull him out. Somebody, in this place this morning. Your misery put you in the uncomfortable place, you've found yourself in. The place of crying, doubt and consistent mistakes and as long as you stay in misery; you'll continually find yourself in the uncomfortable place.

You have to understand, people of God, sometimes we have to go through the uncomfortable, the unclean and the ungodly to get to the place God has for us. If Joseph wouldn't have gone through some hell, he couldn't have made it to the place God had already destined for him.

If Joseph was never sold into slavery, he never would have been sent to Egypt. If he'd never gone to Egypt, he wouldn't have been sold to Potiphar. If he was never sold to Potiphar, he wouldn't have been falsely accused of rape by Potiphar's wife and sent to prison.

If he didn't go to prison, he wouldn't have used his gift of dream interpretation on the baker and butler of Pharaoh? Without interpreting their dreams, he couldn't have interpreted Pharaoh's dreams that took him from prisoner to second in command. Being second in command, put him in position to save his family back in Canaan.

Had Joseph not been placed in an uncomfortable place; he probably wouldn't have amounted to being nothing more than just Jacob's son. But because he'd gone through all of that, he got to the purpose God prepared, long before he was ever thought of.

Somebody, under the sound of my voice; your destiny is waiting and the hell you're facing, the uncomfortable place you're in; is preparing you for it. However, at some point you've got to dismantle the pity party, dry your tears and come out. How? With your praise.

Your mess got you to where you are but your praise can get you out. Yea, while you're down there crouched in the corner of your pit, you need to be yelling out with a mouth and spirit full of praise! Misery may have put you there but praise can get you out. Anybody willing to come out this morning?

I know you may be in your uncomfortable place, at this very moment and you're keeping up appearances for folk but aren't you tired? Come out today, beloved. Allow your praise to free you. Stop worrying about appearances and cry out, from your pit."

"Oh God," I cry out.

"She isn't the only one," I hear him say. "Somebody else needs to be free today."

Mom grabs my hand and I pull back from her.

"Camille, you're not leaving here with this weight. Come on."

Chapter 30

Getting home from church, my entire body is tired from crying. Walking in the front door, we're met by Thomas. I stop.

"Hey son," my dad speaks, embracing him as do mom.

"Daddy," TJ exclaims when they walk in, "I didn't know you were coming."

"I wanted to surprise y'all."

"Are you staying with mom or flying back with us, tomorrow?" Courtney asks.

"We'll talk about that later, okay," he says never taking his eyes off me.

"Come on," mom says to the kids, "and let's see what Chef Jules prepared for dinner."

"Babe," he says walking toward me and I throw my arms around him.

"Thank you for coming."

"You needed me, didn't you?"

"More than you know."

When I release him, we walk upstairs to my bedroom. He closes the door and sits on the bed while I begin to change clothes.

"Camille, I know what you heard Chelle say but baby, I promise I wasn't with her last week."

"Thomas, there is a lot of stuff we need to work through and discuss but right now, I just want to enjoy my family. Can we deal with all of this when we get home?"

He grabs my hand, drawing me to him, kissing my stomach. I raise his head and kiss him on the lips.

"Babe, I miss you."

He wraps his arm around my back and I climb up on him, causing him to lay back.

I stop and lift up.

"I know we have a lot to work out but I need to feel you, please," he begs.

"I was only going to see if you locked the door," I smile.

*****

The kids were supposed to fly back, on Monday to keep from missing days from school but we decided to let them stay until Wednesday.

We took this time to spend with them at Universal Studios, dinners with my parents, golfing with my dad, helping mom with work and having lunch with my aunt.

They all left on Wednesday and since it's my last night here, mom is having a small dinner with Sara, Reese and her husband, Noah.

"Hey," I answer a call from Chloe, putting it on speaker while I finish getting ready.

"Hey, how's Miami?"

"It's been great. How are things there? Wait, you aren't calling to tell me any bad news, are you?"

"No, I was just calling to check on you," she tells me.

"I'm good, girl, enjoying being home."

"You sure?"

"Yes mother, I'm good."

"Okay, you know I worry. It seems to be worse now that I've had the baby. Anyway, I didn't want anything. I'll see you when you get back. Hold up, have you talked to Lyn?"

"Yea, I saw her before I left to come here."

"Ohhh, so you know she's been getting it in with Paul?"

"Getting it in? Who am I talking to because clearly someone has stolen your phone?" I laugh. "Yes, she told me they've being hanging out, again."

"I'm so happy for her because for the first time since everything happened, she's smiling again."

"I know right," I sigh. "I think it's about time for all of us to be happy."

"You sure you're okay?"

"I'm good, just dealing with things before this nomination is announced."

"Girl, you got this. You're one of the strongest chicks I know and if anybody can handle anything, it's you. Don't discount your strength."

"Thanks Chloe."

"You're welcome. Now, I gotta go because Todd is having me watch some Avengers movie while Tamah is asleep."

"Ok sister, enjoy it and I'll see you when I get back."

I press end on the call and look at myself in the mirror.

"Don't discount your strength Camille."

*****

"Ok everybody," I say tapping my glass, once we've all moved into the den. "I know I don't visit, as often as I should but being here this week has really put some things into perspective. I miss y'all, more than I realized and I'm going to do better with coming home. I love everybody in this room and without you all, supporting me, I don't know where I'd be. Now, I'm sure you already know but I'm a possible candidate to fill a vacant position for Circuit Court Judge in my District, back home in Memphis."

"That's my girl," Sara yells, running to give me a hug almost knocking the drink out of my hand.

"This is a huge opportunity and I know it isn't going to be easy but I've learned from the best," I say tipping my glass to my parents, "and I am looking forward to the challenge. In the off chance I do win, I want all of you to come to Memphis to help me celebrate."

"You know I'll be there, honey."

"Momma, why are you acting like she's winning an academy award?" Reese asks, rolling her eyes. "Y'all are always drooling over Cam, like she's royalty. Newsflash, she ain't nothing or nobody."

"Girl, hush hell," her mom tells her.

"No, let her talk auntie so she can finally get whatever it is, off her chest because it's obvious, something is going on. Go on Reese."

"I don't need your permission to speak, bitch," she barks getting up from her seat.

"Hold on heifer," mom says but I look at her, signaling for her to allow Reese to finish.

"Growing up, everything was about you. You got a daddy, who loves you—"

"Aw shit," Sara exclaims, "girl, I knew them damn daddy issues would get you, eventually but baby, you got a daddy too. He ain't wuffadam but you got one."

"It's not just that," she yells, "she always got the attention, from everybody. She was the one with the hips, who all the boys flocked too and I was left with nobody. Let's not forget how she always had to outdo me, graduating early from college and being the top of her law class while I was flunking out. But I bet you never told mommy and daddy, how you actually passed law school."

"Reese, I don't understand where all this is coming from because I've never competed with you and I doggone sure wasn't moved by attention. I passed law school because I worked my ass off to do so. You could have too, if you weren't busy partying."

She chuckles. "Aw, are you still keeping up with that lie?"

"What lie?"

"We both know you didn't work your ass off but you laid on your ass. Go on and tell your parents how you slept with your professors."

"You are a bold face lie," I say moving close to her.

"Am I? So, I didn't see you having sex with Professor Frederick's, in his office, one night?"

Hearing her say his name, stuns me.

"I saw you bent over his desk," she smiles.

"Camille, what is she talking about?" daddy asks.

"Go on Camille and tell them how their precious daughter is really a whore who sleeps her way to the top. I bet you've slept with—"

"SHUT UP," I scream throwing the glass into the wall causing everybody to jump.

"Seems like I ruffled some feathers on the peacock," Reese says laughing. "All this time, you've been celebrated and put on a pedestal when you're nothing more than a common whore."

"Teresa that's enough," her husband bellows.

She continues to taunt. "There's never enough when it comes to the precious Camille. Isn't that right, sister?" Reese mocks as I stumble back to the couch. "Go on, precious and tell the jury your secret."

The room is quiet.

"SAY SOMETHING," Reese yells.

"I was raped."

Chapter 31

"Girl bye, you'd do anything for attention."

I jump off the couch, towards her but dad grabs me.

"I guess you can't handle people knowing that this tough exterior is nothing but a box of shattered glass, huh cousin?"

I scream, trying to get to her.

"Camille, stop," mom yells grabbing my face. "Please, baby, please tell us what happened," she requests with tears in her eyes.

"I didn't sleep with him," I say looking in her eyes. "I didn't sleep with that man."

"Girl," Reese laughs. "I saw you running out of his office—"

"You saw me running from his office because I'd hit him with a paperweight, after he'd forced himself on me."

"Oh baby—"

"No," I say snatching away from them. "This is why I didn't tell y'all. I don't want pity.

"You should have told us," Aunt Sara cries.

"I didn't want y'all looking at me, like you are now. That night, I went to his office, for help on an assignment and afterwards, he forced himself on me. He made me feel worthless and I turned to sex to mask it. I'm so sorry."

Mom comes over then auntie while my dad paces.

"Wow," Reese says, "this girl can tell y'all she turned the sky blue and you'll believe her."

"Let's go," Noah tells her.

"No! Everybody always runs to her rescue but what about me? What about me?"

Sara gets up and walks over to Reese, "girl, I never should have smoked that weed with you, in the seventies because something is wrong with you. This is your cousin."

"So," she spits, "that bitch probably deserved it."

"You need to go," mom tells Reese. "Get out of my house!"

Noah grabs her arm but she pulls away. "No, I'm not going anywhere. Fuck her," she screams as he grabs her up. "Karma's a bitch, bitch. You'll see."

Sara runs after them.

"I'm sorry," I say to my parents. "I should have told y'all when it happened but I was so angry and ashamed."

"I get that Camille but you still should have told us," dad says. "We could have made sure that motherfucker went to jail."

"Jail would have been too easy for him, daddy so I made him pay, my way."

"What did—wait, if you killed him, don't say it."

"I didn't but I wanted to. Instead, I made sure he'd never be able to hurt anybody else." I sit up and take a breath, telling them what happened a few months after the rape.

When I'm done, both of their mouths are opened.

"I knew the rape was the cause of me acting out but I never wanted to face it. Now that you all know, it's time I deal with this. All I ask, is that you all don't treat me any differently."

"Let's pray," mom blurts. "If ever there was a time to call on God, it's now."

We all stand and grab hands.

"Heavenly Father, you're gracious enough to forgive us and merciful enough to not hold our faults against us; thank you. Now God, I need you to saturate this place with your spirit, in order for us to feel your presence. Father, there's some brokenness, in the room that needs to be mended. There're some hearts that need to be healed and a daughter who needs to be made whole.

God, we need you to see about your daughter, Camille. You know what she's had to endure. You've seen what she's been through and you know the deepest, darkest parts of her. Well God, heal now. God, at this very moment, I'm praying for her faith that it will not fail. I'm praying for her mind that it will not be used against her and I'm praying for her joy that it will not be taken.

God, you know. Let her healing start, right now, in this room. Allow her to know that we'd never pity her but we will pick her up. We'd, God, never be ashamed of her but we'll stand in agreement for her healing. God, Thomas is going to need strength to be what she needs on those nights fear will cause her to lash out.

We, her parents and aunt, will need words to encourage her, the times the enemy will speak in her ear. She, God, she will need the courage to face what has happened to her. And while we know, the process of restoration takes time, don't let her faith fail. Then God, while heaven is open and you're listening, heal Teresa because she needs you too. We thank you God and we say, amen."

The next morning, standing at the entrance of the airport, I didn't want to say goodbye to my parents.

Spending time with them this week, made me realize how much I missed being home.

"I love you, baby girl," dad says in my ear making me cry harder, "and you're going to be alright. You have my blood coursing through your veins and that makes you strong enough to come through this. Stay prayed up and stop pushing your husband away. If your marriage can be saved, save it."

"Syl, why are you making this girl cry? Come here," mom says pulling me into her. "When you stop worrying, God can work. You hear me?"

"Yes ma'am."

"Good. Now, you get home and get in therapy. If I find out—"

"I am, I promise."

"Make sure you call me the minute you know something about the nomination." Dad tells me.

"I am sure, you will probably know before me."

"Call me anyway."

"And don't stay away this long again Camille." My mom says.

"I won't. You will be coming to Memphis to plan my celebration party, right?"

"Yes but still."

"I love y'all."

Getting off the airplane, I go to grab my bags from baggage claim. There's a wait so I get my phone to power it back on. Doing so, I begin to get notification after notification.

"What is going on?" I mumble.

I see a text from Ray with a link.

RAY: Bitch, you are a superstar now!

I click the link.

"The Shelby County Judicial Commission has just released the names of three attorneys who have been nominated to fill the vacant seat left by Circuit Court Judge Sumner, who retired due to illness.

The commission has nominated attorney Aubrey Holman, attorney Patrick Kenlee and attorney

Camille Shannon. Governor Lee will select one, of the three finalists who will then fill the seat until the next general election."

My hand flies to my mouth, "oh my God," I say as tears fill my eyes.

My phone rings, pausing the video.

"Daddy, yes, I just saw it. Yes sir, thank you. No, I'm waiting on my bags. Okay. I love you too."

I walk in a circle, in shock, scrolling through the other texts.

SHELBY: Oh my God!! I'm so proud of you.

CHLOE: I never had a doubt. Now, we wait for you to be selected.

LYN: Sister!!!

KERRI: (crying emoji) I'm so proud of you.

COURTNEY: You are my SHERO!

I dial Thomas' number but he doesn't answer. Instead he sends a text.

THOMAS: Can't answer but I saw the news. Will call once I'm done.

I don't reply and instead drop my phone in my purse because trying to go through the rest of these messages will have me missing my bags.

Chapter 32

When I get to my car, in short term parking, I look at my watch and it's almost five o'clock. I decide to stop by Dr. Scott's office. I don't know if she's available but if not, I'll schedule an appointment.

I walk into the office but there's no receptionist, at the front desk. I wait a few minutes before I go back to Dr. Scott's office. The door is cracked and there's music playing. I knock but there's no answer.

I may be broken but you are welcome. I may need your healing and I say you're welcome. I know you are able, in spite of how I feel. You are welcome.

Please God, we need you to have your way. You are welcome. It's not just enough to welcome Him, you have to give Him permission. Tell God, you are welcome. You are welcome, God, have your way.

Listening to the words of the song, I begin to back away from the door.

"Camille."

I turn to see Dr. Scott.

"That song," I say with tears in my eyes.

"It's called, 'You are Welcome' by Psalmist Raine. Beautiful, isn't it?"

I nod.

"I like to listen to music, in between patients as a way to soak the room with God's presence. You never know what a person is going through and if they can feel God, by stepping in my office then so shall it be."

She goes over and stops the music.

"Have a seat and tell me what's wrong."

"I didn't mean to bother you and if you don't have time, I can make an appointment."

"Camille, stop running," she says when I make it to the door. "Dang girl, aren't you tired? How can you ever heal, if all you do is run?"

"If I stop, I might not survive," I tell her.

"How would you know? Look, I have about thirty minutes before my next appointment and it's apparent you need them, or you wouldn't be here."

I walk over and sit.

"You're here Camille and in this place, in the midst of God's anointing; you're safe. Allow Him to do the work."

"I've been nominated to fill an empty seat as a judge," I tell her, wringing my hands together.

"That's great news, isn't it?"

"It is but," I take a deep breath, "my life is a mess."

"Camille, a mess can be cleaned up. Why don't you start by telling me about this mess?"

"I was raped and I don't know how to forgive myself," I blurt.

"What exactly are you forgiving yourself for?"

"I don't know," I say, frustrated. "All these years, I've held on to this secret and now that people know, I don't want them to treat me any differently. I'm not someone who needs pity."

"Is that what you've gotten when you tell people?"

"No but—"

"You're making excuses, Camille."

"Excuses?" I ask, confused.

"Truth is, you don't have a reason not to forgive yourself but you're afraid when you forgive you, you're going to lose Cam. She's the person who protects Camille from being hurt again, the one who seeks out men, she can control with her sexuality because she has to be in control. Cam is your security blanket but she's also the reason you're suffering and until you let her go, you'll always find yourself in a dark place."

"How can I let her go? She's the one who got me through this."

"No, she's the one who got you to this because you haven't gotten through anything. Camille, you're still fighting against being healed. Why?"

"This, she is all I know. The nights I wanted to kill myself, she stopped me."

"Camille, she may have stopped you from killing yourself but you're still dying, on the inside. Cam, this fictitious wall, you've created, hasn't stopped you from hurting yourself. Truth is, all she's done, was change the terms."

"What do you mean?"

"Cam stopped you from committing suicide but she replaced a physical death with a mental death. Either way, the people you love, have still lost you. Instead of a physical death, they're experiencing an emotional death which is much harder. At least with a physical death, there's some finality."

"Are you saying my family would have been better off, had I killed myself?"

"Is that what you heard because that's not, at all, what I said. Camille—"

"Why can't you call me Cam?"

"That's not your name. Camille when a person dies a physical death, the family mourns but can usually find some ray of peace, after the funeral because things are final. However with an emotional death, every time they see you, suffering, knowing there's nothing they can do to help you, there is no ray of hope. They experience you dying, over and over again. How old are you Camille?"

"Thirty-nine."

"Too damn old to still be hiding behind Cam."

I'm taken back by her words and tone.

"Does that hurt your feelings? Good, because it's about time you come out from behind this veil of shame. Camille, you aren't the first person who has gone through this and neither are you the first to use some reckless method of covering up."

"Then what do I do?"

"You have to release Cam."

"How?"

"By forgiving and embracing Camille because you may just find you like the person, she is." She looks at her watch. "I have another client, coming in but Camille, today you made a step in the right direction but in order to heal, you've got to go all the way. I'd like you to try something."

"What's that?"

"I want you to spend a weekend with me."

"As in, more than an hour?"

"Yes. It's what I call, the Hagar Experience, created on the foundation of Genesis 16, verses seven through ten."

She gets up and goes over to get a brochure.

"Hagar was the servant of Sarai and Abram. Sarai was old and without children so she decided to give Abram, Hagar to impregnate with a child. Yet, after Hagar got pregnant, she started to disrespect Sarai. Sarai then had Hagar cast into the wilderness, pregnant and alone."

"That was her fault," I tell her.

"Sure, Hagar is partly to blame yet, none of this would have happened hadn't Sarai messed with God's plan for their lives. However, while Hagar was in the wilderness, she is met by God who promised her something. He told her, if she went back to the place that caused her the agony, of being in the wilderness, He'd give her more descendants than she could count."

"How is this supposed to help me?"

"Camille, you're in the wilderness because you were cast out by your actions, caused by something you didn't ask for. Going through the Hagar Experience, it is my hope that you'll see that God promises, toward you, are still good. First, you have to go back and face what caused this agony, in the first place. Take some time to think about it and if you want to do it, call me."

As soon as I walk out of Dr. Scott's office, I get to the car and find an envelope on my windshield. I open it to find my medical records from being in the hospital. I flip through the pages and see the reports of cocaine in my system and a note that says, **IS THIS A FUTURE JUDGE? DROP OUT OR I LEAK YOUR SECRET. YOU HAVE ONE WEEK.**

I get in the car and throw the envelope on the seat, "and so it begins."

I get home and Thomas surprises me at the door. Pulling me into a hug. "What's wrong?" he questions when he lets me go.

"This," I say, handing him the envelope. He begins to flip through it.

"Where did you get this?"

"It was left on my windshield when I left from seeing my therapist, Dr. Scott"

"Dr. Scott? What happened to Dr. Nelson?"

"That isn't important but this is," I point to the papers. "This could destroy every chance I have of getting the seat. You need to get your baby momma in check."

"Hold up, how would Chelle get this information? Nobody but us, knew what you were in the hospital for."

"Unless you told her, during one of—"

"Don't go there Camille because you know I'd never do anything like that. Besides, I don't think Chelle could pull this off."

"Who else has a reason?"

"I don't know but maybe you should think about pulling out of the nomination."

"Are you serious?"

"I'm only offering a suggestion. Look, let's figure this out."

"You suggest I drop out of the nomination but you don't have a suggestion as it relates to Chelle? Got it." I get up and go to the guest room where I undress and get in the shower.

"God, I'm not perfect and haven't always been right but I'm trying. Can you please reveal my enemies and deal with them accordingly? If this position is meant for me, give me the strength to endure what's to come. Amen."

Chapter 33

Sunday Morning

I decide to go to High Point, for service. We're late but we're here. The kids are with me but they decided to go to the youth side. I walk in and sit in the back of the church as Pastor Reeves is already up.

"It is time we take the blinders off our eyes, it's time we come out the dark and it's time we check ourselves. There are too many Godly women showing up to worship, accepting what folk is shoving down your throat because it's safe and sweet only to leave here still bound and more confused.

There are too many of God's children, who have grown up in the church and still haven't matured spiritually. There are too many of God's children dressed up but tore up. You're smiling but secretly suicidal, looking happy but heart full of hate, able but too angry to let go and fighting everything you come into contact with because it hurts you to forgive.

Yes ma'am, yes sir; we can pray for God to give us a discerning heart but it might be too much if you are not ready for it. We can pray for discernment all day and night, get it and it can blow our minds. Why? Because when we should be, spiritually, digesting the meat of God's word, a lot of us are still lapping up the milk because we are too afraid to shake up the contents of the bottle.

For the author of Hebrews says it like this, in Hebrews 5:14, *"But solid food is for the mature, for those who have their powers of discernment trained by constant practice to distinguish good from evil.""*

"Preach pastor," someone yells.

"Beloved, I didn't come to slay you in the spirit, I came that you might be saved. I didn't show up to let you see how cute I look in my skirt, there are some folk who needs to shift spiritually. I didn't show up to badger you but I came because some folks need the blinders removed from their eyes.

I didn't come to prove to anybody my gift, I came so God can get the glory and He told me to tell you to be careful what you pray for because He gives what we ask for in faith. Please understand, I am not trying to place fear into your heart neither am I trying to steer you away from what you are looking to do.

However, I wouldn't be who God has called me to be, if I am not being obedient to who He is and the message in which He gives. And He says be careful what you ask for. Be careful what you pray for because a discerning heart has the ability to show you the trueness of some stuff. Again, you don't have to be afraid of the gift of discernment but you need to be able to handle it.

Simply stating, discernment can be given but you keep it by consistently working God's word, by not being afraid to tell the difference between right and wrong and boldly calling out the good from evil. You cannot do that being comfortable, lazy and being talked out of your position.

This is why we are good with striving to be the Proverbs 31 woman and yet the only time we speak on the qualities of a Godly woman is annual days. Yes, we feel good when somebody is telling you how to get your Boaz but how will you know what he looks like if you can't tell the difference between Righteous Richard and Trifling Tyrone.

This is why you have to be careful what you pray for. For the bible says in *Hebrews 4:12, "For the word of God is quick and powerful and sharper than any two-edged sword, piercing even to the dividing asunder of soul and spirit and of the joints and marrow and is a discerner of the thoughts and intents of the heart."*

This means when you pray for discernment, you'll find yourself being put to sleep, one night, in the middle of your bedroom floor and God doing surgery on your heart. His word will begin to pierce the mechanics of your body and it'll start to make you feel differently. You'll start to see things moving away from you that you won't even reach for, this time.

You'll start to see some things being shook up in your life that you won't even bother with trying to fix this time. You'll see some folk walk out that you won't even chase after this time."

I'm on the edge of my seat, as I listen to this sermon piercing parts of me.

"What are you seeking?" she asks. "What are you searching for? What are you trying to grasp? What beloved? If it's fame among folk, be careful what you pray for. If it's the approval of man, be careful what you pray for.

But if you are truly ready then pray like Solomon did in *First Kings 3:9*, *"Give your servant therefore an understanding mind to govern your people that I may discern between good and evil, for who is able to govern this your great people?"*

For I showed up this morning feeling like Paul must have felt in *First Corinthians 2 when* he says, *"I didn't come with big words and fancy titles but I came, leaving all of me by the mercy of the living God. With a plain message and the power of the Holy Spirit."*

This is why no eyes have seen neither ears heard, or minds can understand what God has for those of us who love Him. Be careful what you pray for."

She begins to repeat that as the music begins to play.

"The doors of God's house are open. Is there someone here who needs God to perform surgery on them? Someone who has been praying for God to reveal some things but in the back of your mind, you're afraid of what it may show? If you're here and you've lost your connection to God, you can come."

My leg is shaking as I stand but I can't do it. Instead, I walk out the door.

Chapter 34

The next morning, I walk into the office.

"Camille," Stephanie squeals when I walk in, "Congratulations."

"Thank you."

"How was your trip?"

"It was great and it felt good being home. It also made me realize how much I miss my mom and dad."

"Being that far away from them has to be hard."

"It is," I sigh. "Anyway, how has it been around here?"

"Quiet, until your name was released and since it's been crazy. You've had a lot of people stop by. Judge Alton called and Mr. Townsend is waiting for you in his office."

"Already?"

"Yes ma'am. He's been here since about six."

"Okay," I exhale. "Wait, has Raul been here because I was expecting a report from him, while I was gone?"

"He's been out of the office. His wife went into labor early but he's due back today."

"Can you tell him I need to see him?"

"Sure thing."

I put my bags in my office and make my way to Mr. Townsend's. Anita, his admin, is at her desk and she waves me in.

"Camille," Mr. Townsend says with a huge smile on his face. "Congratulations. I talked to your dad this morning and he is so excited."

"I know," I laugh, "he's called me a few times."

"Have a seat. Are you excited?"

"Excited, nervous, anxious and everything else you can think of."

"That's normal but you'll be okay."

"How long do you think it will be before Governor Lee makes his announcement?"

"I have it on good authority that he'll make it within the next two to three weeks, because he wants the seat filled," he says when someone taps on the door. "Come in"

"Good morning sir," a young woman says.

"Good, you're just in time. Camille, this is Carin Shields. She's a publicist, I use from time to time."

"Good Morning, Camille. I've heard so many good things about you."

"Good morning, thank you and it's nice to meet you."

"Camille, I've asked Carin to come in to prepare a press release to send to all the major media outlets. We've had a lot of calls since the news released your name."

"This will not be a full press kit, just something to give them a sense of who you are. However, I will have to put together a full one, soon to include headshots, a few photos of your family and information on your law history. I'll set up a time to get the photos done."

"What else?" I ask.

"In the meantime, if you are approached by any media, refer them to me. Here's my card."

"Wait, I did get a call from a lady at channel 2 News while I was in Miami. She was asking questions about me being nominated and some personal business that she shouldn't have known."

"What was her name?"

"Um, Lauren, I think."

"What type of personal information did she have?"

I look at Mr. Townsend and he nods. "You can be open and honest with her."

"My husband has been having an affair and may have a baby on the way. She knew this which means someone has been feeding her information. Also, last night when I was leaving my therapist's office, there was an envelope on my car that included some medical records and—"

"What is it?" she asks.

"Almost a year ago, I accidentally overdosed on cocaine. I didn't know that's what it was, at the time and only found out, after waking up in the hospital. I'm sorry, Mr. Townsend, I know I should have told you this but—"

"I knew," he says, cutting me off. "I knew when it happened. Thomas told me."

"You never said anything."

"And I wouldn't have unless you showed me that I needed too," he tells me.

"Is there anything else?" Carin asks.

"No that's it but the note said I had a week to drop out the race or they would leak it to the media."

"I'll deal with that," she says typing something in her phone. "Are you and your husband getting a divorce?"

"No, we're trying to work things out," I reply.

"Where is the envelope?"

"In my office."

"Does anyone else know about this?"

"Just my husband and whoever left it," I tell her.

"I'll stop by and get it on my way out but are you sure there's nothing else I need to know about?"

"Not unless there is something else you can think of to ask."

"Not at the moment but if there is anything else, I'll call you and if you think of anything, call me at any time."

"Thank you, Ms. Shields and Mr. Townsend."

I make it back to my office and get all of the information together for Carin. I finally get a chance to sit down at my computer to check my email when I see a reminder for Monica's book release party and it reminds me to send a text to the girls.

I get my phone and send a group text to them. Pressing send, I hear a knock on the door and look up to see Carin. I close my laptop and stand up to meet her.

"Hey, here's the envelope."

"Thanks."

"Carin, do you think this will hurt my chance at being selected? The note said, I had a week to drop out or this would be leaked to the media."

"I'm not going to lie; this can potentially be bad but let me work my magic which may include you making a statement. All I ask is for you to trust me. Can you do that?" she inquires.

"Yes."

"Trust, between us, means no secrets," she reiterates.

"I got it."

"Camille, I've worked with Mr. Townsend for over ten years and I know when he believes in someone. He's placed his name on the line for you and if you aren't ready or capable of handling some bad press, bow out now."

"I can handle it."

"I believe you can but believing and doing are two different things. Now, do you have any idea who would be sending you these things?"

"I think it's the chick who's pregnant by my husband because a rock was thrown through my window, a couple weeks ago. It had a childish note that said, karma is a bitch—wait," I pause. "Reese."

"Who is Reese?" Carin asks.

"My cousin," I tell her, trying to remember what she said.

"No, I'm not going anywhere. Fuck her," she screams *as he grabs her up.* *"Karma's a bitch, bitch! You'll see."*

"Do you think she could be involved? Why?" she inquires

"Because she said the same thing to me when I was home this past week but how can she do any of this and she's in Miami?" I ask, thinking out loud.

"Is Reese her full name?" Carin questions.

"No, it's Teresa Cortez but she's married now and I don't know her new last name, we aren't that close but I'll get it and call you."

"Do that but in the meantime, you need to focus on doing what you do best which is your job and let me handle the rest."

"Oh, I did ask Raul, my investigator to look into Chelle but I haven't had a chance to follow up with him," I tell her.

"I'll get with him but again, if you need me; don't hesitate to call. You can reach me at any time, day or night."

She leaves and I start to work through a few emails when I get an instant message from Raul saying he's heading to my office.

"Hey," he taps on the door, "I'm sorry I didn't get a chance to get back to you sooner."

"It's cool. Stephanie told me Carissa had the baby. How are they?"

"They are both doing good," he says pulling out his phone to show me a picture.

"Oh Raul, he is handsome."

"Thank you. I think I did pretty good," he smirks and I shake my head.

"Spoken like a true big-headed man."

He laughs, taking a seat. "I got some information on Michelle Craft. I gave Carin a copy of this too because she said, you wouldn't mind."

"No, it's cool."

"Okay, well I ran a background and financial check on her and she has a few petty charges, for traffic tickets and some shoplifting but nothing recent. Financially, this chick is a few pennies from bankruptcy which is bad because she's already filed twice, in the last five years."

"Do you think she's a threat?"

"You can never tell what a person will or won't do. All I know, this chick is strapped for cash and you know the lengths people will go through for money."

"Yea, I know. Thank you, Raul."

"No problem. I'll send you all the information I have, including her phone records and social media stuff when I get back to my office. Do you want me to continue to look into her?"

"No, this should be enough. Thanks, Raul."

When he leaves, I sit back in my chair trying to figure out, who could be behind this, if it isn't Chelle. Reese, possibly but what would she have to gain.

"This doesn't make sense," I say out loud.

I push that to the back of my mind, while I try to get some work done.

Chapter 35

A few days later, I'm standing in the mirror, in my closet, trying to decide if what I have on, is okay.

"Damn girl," Thomas says from the door.

"You don't think it's too young, looking?" I ask, referring to the jean overalls I've paired with a white knit shirt, dark blue blazer and heels.

"No, you look amazing. Where are you headed?"

"To a book release party for one of my clients. I told you about it, remember."

"Oh," he says.

"Thomas—"

"Babe, go and have fun. I'll be waiting on you when you get home." He walks over and kisses me on the forehead.

"Divas! Are you ready to party?" I ask walking into Shelby's house, a half hour later.

"Hell yes," Ray says acting like she's twerking.

"Then let's ride."

It feels good to be heading out with the girls because it's been a while and we're all overdue for a night of fun. I'm in Thomas' truck because it had room for all of us.

Parking, outside the venue, I don't turn the truck off.

"Before we go in, there's something I have to tell y'all. Thomas has been having an affair."

The truck gets eerily quiet.

"With Chelle and she's pregnant."

"Aw hell no, I know you are freaking lying? Thomas, shirt buttoned up to the top, always got his nose turned up about something, is cheating?" Ray asks.

"Yep and I think she's trying to sabotage my chance at getting the position."

"Cam, why haven't you told us this?" Kerri asks.

"I've been trying to process everything. Mr. Townsend hired a publicist, who's taking care of the press stuff but I wanted you all to know, in case you are contacted by anyone."

"Listen boo, we got you," Chloe tells me. "This is only the devil trying to stop what's for you. Well, he can't because we'll go to war with him, about you."

"Chloe is right," Shelby adds, "and I think this is a great time to get with Pastor Magnolia—"

"No—"

"Girl, hush. You need somebody oily and spiritual attached to you and that's Pastor Magnolia. I know you're going through but there's no better time, than the present to rebuild your faith."

"Okay," I relent, sighing.

"Good, because I've already been texting her and she'll meet with us tomorrow afternoon, at my house."

I look at her and she shrugs, before opening the door. I can't help but laugh and shake my head before turning off the truck and going inside. When we make it in, the party is in full swing and it is very nice. I notice Monica who is waving me over to her.

"Camille, I'm so glad you could make it. You look great."

"Thank you and you do, as well. Let me introduce you to my best friends," I tell her. "This is Shelby, Raylan, Kerri, Lyn and Chloe."

"Hello ladies, it is so nice to meet you and thank you for coming tonight. Babe," she says to Brent, "look who's here."

When he turns, I see who he's talking too.

"Chelle?"

"You two know each other?" Monica asks.

"Not really," I reply.

"Of course, we do," she smiles. "We share the same penis, occasionally."

"Uh—" Monica says but I interrupt.

"No, what she means is, she buys time with the penis that I own. Isn't that right, Chelle?"

Her face gets red and she walks off. I turn to Brent who is trying to keep from laughing. "Mr. Prosecutor, how are you?"

"I, um, I'm great Camille and it's good to see you. Hello ladies," he says to the girls, "can I get you all something to drink?"

"Yes," Ray says, "some wine would be great."

When he walks off, Monica is telling Chloe about her latest book and that she'll be doing a reading, from it, in about thirty minutes. Meanwhile, I'm mean mugging Chelle.

"Come on," Ray says pulling me away. We find an empty table, before heading to get some food. Getting back to the table, Brent has left a bottle of wine and glasses for us.

We take our seats, as Monica gets up to speak.

"Hello everybody," she says into the microphone. "I'm so grateful to each of you for coming out tonight for the release of my newest book, Obsession. I'm going to read a couple of paragraphs, you can buy a few copies, snap a few selfies and then we can party."

Chapter 36

She sits on a stool and begins to read.

"This is the first chapter, told from Khris, spelled K-H-R-I-S' perspective.

I walk in the house after a long day at work. Darius hasn't made it in yet so I take a quick shower and throw on some lounging clothes before starting dinner.

As I am pulling the cornbread from the oven, he walks in.

"What's up boo? Girl, you got it smelling good in here," he says walking over to the stove. "Dang, is that your homemade mac and cheese? You must be trying to get some from a brotha?"

"Dude, if you don't go shower so we can eat. I'm starving."

"Say no mo," he says, running from the kitchen. I laugh and shake my head while getting two plates from the cabinet. I fix us both a healthy serving of fried chicken, mac

and cheese, green beans and corn bread. I grab two glasses and the pitcher of tea. Fifteen minutes later he comes in wearing only jogging pants and I look him up and down. He sees me staring and smile.

"Really D?"

"What? You don't think you'll be able to concentrate with all this chocolate on display?" he asks rubbing his hand from his neck to the top of his pants. "Don't worry, daddy will give you dessert later."

"Boy, sit down," I laugh. "How was your day? I drove by the shop this morning, on my way to work and you were already extremely busy."

"Yea with this week's sale on rims, we've had nonstop action. Thank you for coming up with all the marketing and everything. Had it not been for you, we wouldn't have half the sales."

"Babe, you don't have to thank me for helping you. We're in this together, right?"

"Of course," he says kissing me. "How was your day and the meeting with a new client?"

"Yea but I don't know if I'm going to take her on."

"Since when are you turning down clients?"

"It was something about her."

"Really Khris?"

"I'm serious D. There was something about her that felt off. It was like she came into the office just to find out about me. It was weird."

"What did she ask you to do?"

"She owns a few preschools, in the city and wants me to take their holiday photos but I just don't know."

"Babe, this could be the break you need. Are you sure you want to turn that down? A daycare could be great to add to your growing list of clients."

"I know but grandma told me, all money isn't good money."

"Yea, well grandma don't have the bills we have either."

I give him the side eye and he shrug.

"I haven't turned it down yet but I'm going to pray about it and if God leads, I'll take her on. Otherwise, it's a no from me."

"What was so wrong with this chick and have you looked her up on social media" he asks getting up for more food.

"Not yet and nothing was physically wrong with her. She is actually a very beautiful lady but it was her vibe. She made me feel like I had something of hers and she was coming to get it back. Come to think of it, she was really interested in our wedding photos. Let me find out she's one of your old thots."

"Girl, you're the only thot I want," he says before laughing, loud.

"Keep playing and this will be your last meal before the funeral home gives you your last bath."

"Babe, you watch too many of those Lifetime movies." He says when he is done laughing. "What's her name?"

"Tiffany Patterson."

He chokes.

"Do you know her?"

"I dated a Tiffany Patterson, in college but this couldn't be the same one."

"Why not?"

"She died, our senior year," he says.

"Naw, this one is very much alive but she's still creepy. Anyway, have you decided on your costume for Sami's Halloween Party."

"Yep, I'm going as a stallion."

I choke on my tea before I burst into laughing. "Dude!"

"What? All I have to do is walk in with this chest out and all the attention will be on me."

"Well, you will not be walking in beside me with that bird chest uncovered."

"I ain't going as no bar of soap either," he tells me stuffing his mouth with food.

"Why not? It'll be cute. Me as a loofah sponge and--"

"And nothing," he cuts me off. "Think of something else babe."

"Fine!"

We finish dinner and he move to the couch while I clean the kitchen. After I'm done, I walk into the living room to see him sprawled out on the couch with a cigar in his hand.

I go over to the sound system and turn on pandora. As the sound of Tank's 'When We' engulfs the room, I close my eyes and begin moving to the music. When I open them, I see him watching me and it turns me on. I start removing my clothes before walking back to the couch, straddling him.

I take the cigar from his hand and place it in the ash tray on the table. I kiss him on the forehead before moving down to the tip of his nose and then his mouth. I release his lips and move down to his chest, making a trail to his stomach with my tongue. When I get to the top of his pants, he gasps from the feel of my breath.

"You did say something about dessert, right?"

When we are done, we both exhale our pleasure. I smile at him and he grabs me, flipping us both off the couch. When he hits the floor with me on top, his eyes are closed.

"Um, did you forget we were on the couch?" I ask laughing before kissing him and getting up. I grab my clothes and walk into the bathroom to wash up.

Throwing my shorts into the hamper, I walk out of the bathroom to Darius running into the bedroom.

"Babe, put on some clothes, we got to go," he stammers.

"Go where? What's wrong?"

"My shop, it's on fire!"

Chapter 37

"Wow," we all say when she's done.

"Okay, you'll have to buy the book to see how things work out for Khris and Darius and the real reason behind the name Obsession."

Once everyone is done clapping, I turn to see Lyn, head down into her phone.

"Um, Lynesha Williams, what has you grinning at that phone like that?"

"Nothing, laughing at Paul."

"Paul, huh?" Shelby inquires. "Are y'all back together?"

"Right now, we're just enjoying each other's company. We've started having civilized conversations again but the other night, he came over," she says drawing out the word came.

"And? Heifer, spill it," Kerri orders.

"Let's just say, I slept for the first time, in a long time."

"That's what I'm talking about," I exclaim.

"It's about time for us to smile again," Shelby says. "I didn't think it was possible, the weeks after Brian passed away but I'm finding that it is."

Ray grabs her hand.

"Speaking of smiling, did you go to lunch with Dr. Hotty," I ask Shelby.

"Yes and it was good but I can't lie, I felt guilty."

"Guilty about what?"

"It hasn't been long since Brian has been gone and I didn't want to be looking like a hoe in these streets."

"A what?" I ask, choking on my wine.

"I saw that on Instagram," she laughs. "Seriously, I did feel guilty but now, I'm allowing God to work out everything, in His time."

"That's all you can do," Kerri tells her, "and while we're on the subject of good news, I'm pregnant."

"Oh my God, Kerri," we all say. "Wait, you are happy, right?"

"Yes, like Shelby said, it's time we all smile again."

As soon as the words leave Shelby's mouth, I look up to see Chelle talking to Brent.

"Cam, you okay?"

"Yea but I'm trying to figure out what Chelle's game is."

"Well, we ain't finding out tonight, let's dance," Ray says, standing to grab my arm when the Wobble, line dance begins to play.

After a few line dances, more wine, taking pictures and purchasing books from Monica; we prepare to leave.

Getting to the truck, Chelle is standing there.

"Girl, what do you want?" I ask.

"Cam, I didn't come here to argue with you. Can we talk?"

"Boo, there's nothing for us to talk about. Please leave me alone."

"Or what?" she asks crossing her arms. "or what? Huh? What are you going to do to me Camille Shannon? I only wanted to talk to your stuck-up ass."

People stop to look at her.

"Didn't you just get nominated for a city position?" she smiles.

"Girl, why are you doing all this freaking screaming?" Shelby questions, as we stand there and look at her. "Do you need attention because from the looks of it, you're getting it so you can cut the act."

"Why are y'all bothering me?" she yells again. "This is my man's truck and I was waiting for him."

"Y'all, let's go." I tell them.

"Yes, I think that's best," she says, lowering her voice and with a smirk. "I'd hate for something to happen to your precious nomination. Oh, I saw your picture on the news. You were cute."

I lunge at her.

"No," Ray yells, "there are people videoing."

"Yea," Lyn remarks, "don't hit her because you have too much to lose for choking this hoe. Me though, I'm overdue for a night in jail." She snatches Chelle by the hair, dragging her around to the front of the truck. "Trick, you need to leave."

"Go ahead and hit me, because I'm pregnant," she taunts. "Give the people a show. Why are you mad at me, I didn't tell your husband to get me pregnant," she continues to scream. "Let me go!"

"Lyn, let her go. She isn't worth it."

"That's not what our husband says, especially the nights, I send him home happy," she taunts fixing her breasts that have popped out of her bra.

"Girl, if you think, for a moment, I'm bothered by you giving Thomas head, inside his truck, think again. If anything, you ought to be concerned with the fact, you aren't even worth a $35 hotel room for an hour. Baby bye but I'll be sure to let Thomas know when I get home."

"I don't need you letting him know nothing," she yells, "I can call him myself."

"You do that."

"Yea run like you always do," she laughs. "Isn't that what you're good at Camille, running? Then why don't you run along and leave our man alone because I can handle all that."

I turn back.

"No Cam," Lyn says.

"I'm not going to touch this slut but let me explain something to you, Chelle. It's obvious, you don't have anything to lose, including a baby because no person, in their right mind, would be standing out here like this. Look at you, beloved. You're making a fool of yourself and for what? Some Facebook live fame? Girl, get yourself together. Ladies, let's go."

"I, I don't know what to say," Shelby says, once we've driven off and left Chelle standing there, screaming.

"Me either," I tell them, gripping the steering wheel because I'm fuming.

"Cam calm down boo. You drive fast when you're mad."

"I'm sorry, y'all," I reply, taking a breath and slowing down. "He keeps telling me, he's no longer messing with her but why else would she do this."

"She's a lunatic. No other way to explain it."

"You're right," I relent, "but his ass has some explaining to do."

I make it home, after dropping the girls off. I walk into our bedroom and Thomas is asleep. My phone begins to go off in my hand. I open it to Facebook notifications.

"Hey," I shake him. "Hey, you need to get up."

"Hey babe, how was the party?"

"Are you still fooling with Chelle? Be honest Thomas because I am not in the mood for anything other than that."

"No, I told you that I haven't been with Chelle. Why are you asking me about her?"

I throw my phone at him before going into my closet to undress. I walk out to him staring at the phone.

"Babe—"

"No, save it Thomas. Look, I don't know what's going on with you and Chelle but one of us has a problem. Either Chelle does, for all the stunts she's pulling or me for believing you when you say there's nothing going on."

"Baby, I promise, there's nothing going on with us. I don't know what would possess her to do this."

My phone dings again. I grab it from him.

"Do you see this? Somebody has already tagged me in this shit. Do you not understand how bad this could be, for me?"

"Why is everything always about you? Hell, I told you I don't know why she would do this but not every freaking thing is about you, Camille."

"Are you serious? My name was just released as one of three possible nominees to fill Judge Sumner's seat, not even a week ago and now this?"

"Maybe you should think about dropping out?"

"What?"

"Listen to me, for a moment. With everything going on this may not be a good time for your name to be in the race. You can remove your name and that way; we'll have more time to repair our marriage. We can go to counseling, take a vacation and spend the rest of this year; relearning each other."

"Dude, I don't need to relearn you. I need your baby momma to back the hell off and if you have a problem with me being in the race, why would you wait until now to say it?"

"I don't have a problem. I'm proud of you, Camille, you know this but couldn't this just be, the wrong time?"

"I'm going to take a shower and then I'm sleeping back in the guestroom."

"Babe—"

I walk in and slam the door.

Chapter 38

The next afternoon, we're all in Shelby's living room when the doorbell rings. She goes to answer it and comes back with Pastor Magnolia Reeves and Rev. Denise French.

"Hello ladies," they say.

We all speak and they take their seats. Shelby has water, juice and wine out, along with sausage, cheese and crackers.

"Okay," Shelby says, "I asked all of us to come together this afternoon for prayer, release and guidance. A lot has happened to us and I believe we're at a point of needing to be renewed. Seeing that we're all trying to find our ways back from pain, suffering, loss and everything else; we can't do this without God."

"Amen," Ray chimes in.

"Before we begin, let's pray," Rev. French says. "Father God, we thank you for time spent in communion with you. God, we thank you for allowing us to make it here this afternoon to be in fellowship with your children. We don't know what they stand in need of but God give us the power, wisdom and right discernment to be what they need.

Speak through us, today, turning this living room into your hospital of restoration. Speak through us so that nobody leaves here the same way they came. Speak through us, Father so that you get the glory and not us. For we're just your servants. Move us out of the way so your children may be renewed and their faith restored. Thank you, God for what you're going to allow to transpire, in this sacred place. Amen."

We all say amen.

"Shelby, we thank you for allowing us, in your home," Pastor Reeves says. "Each of you have to understand, being here, today, will not right every one of your wrongs and neither will it be the answer to every problem. Truthfully, being here may open you up to be attacked because the enemy doesn't want you free.

However, when you trust God through everything, He'll protect you. The Bible shares in Lamentations three, twenty-two and twenty-three; *"the steadfast love of the Lord never ceases, His mercies never come to an end; they are new every morning but great is your faithfulness."* Even after hearing that God grants us new mercies, every morning this scripture ends with great is your faithfulness.

Faithfulness means, true, devoted, constant and dependable. See, God is dependable, showing up every morning to give us new mercies when most of us haven't been faithful to nobody or nothing. God shows up, every morning, faithfully yet some of us rarely speak to Him. God gives us, new mercies, what we don't deserve, every morning."

"Why though? If most of us don't deserve it, why does He do it?" I ask. "I'm having a hard time coming to grips with that. Why would He do that for us?"

"Because it's His reputation on the line. You're Camille, right?"

I nod.

"Congratulations on your nomination but you're in for a fight. You know why? The enemy isn't ready to let you go yet and if he can continue to block you from hearing God, he'll do it. If the enemy can stop you from crying out to God, he'll do it. Crazy thing, you started to pray again, didn't you?"

I nod.

"And your attacks got heavier, didn't they?"

I nod again, wiping tears.

"Where is your faithfulness Camille?"

"Why are you only talking to me?" I lash out.

"Because you're the one God is talking to, right now. You can fight me but I'm not going anywhere because then the enemy wins."

"I don't mean any harm, pastor but sometimes it feels like God doesn't listen to somebody like me."

"Somebody like you? What makes you different from any of us? My sister, God hears you, every time you call Him, whether you're in sin or not," she replies.

"Then why won't he answer?"

"He answers and when you stop running, you'll hear Him. Camille, how many more nights are you going to spend, tossing and turning? How many more days are you going to lose, feeling like you aren't good enough? How many more moments, are you going to devote to denying your gifts? How many more Sundays are you going to miss out on connecting with Him?"

I stand up.

"Do you not understand that God doesn't use us because He needs us? Baby, God can make rocks cry out and donkeys talk yet He finds favor in us and because He finds us favored; He'll send us to do things man says we shouldn't. At this very moment, you don't feel worthy of walking in the thing you've prayed and prepared for, all your life; why not?"

I look around the room, at the girls.

"What are you so afraid of?"

"Failing," I answer.

"You think God will intentionally set you up to fail? Think about it, Camille. Why would God call you out of the darkness, give you new mercies, set you apart from most and deem you worthy; at this very moment; just so you can fail? If He did, His reputation would be tainted and people wouldn't believe and trust Him anymore. People believe God by testing God. What you're going through, it isn't personal baby this is God's business and you have to let Him do what He does."

"I don't feel worthy," I cry. "I'm broken but more than anything, I'm exhausted."

"That's shattered," Rev. French states.

I look at her.

"What you just said is the definition of shattered. Here's what the word says," she tells me pulling out her phone. "The Message Bible translates First Peter, four and nineteen like this, *"So if you find life difficult because you're doing what God said, take it in stride. Trust Him. He knows what He's doing and He'll keep on doing it."* So, what if you're broken, we've been there. So, what if you're exhausted, hell, we've all been there. The question now is, what are you going to do about it?" Rev. French looks at me.

"Camille, you are as worthy as you believe you are. Your mistakes don't discount the anointing. Here's what I know," Pastor Magnolia says, moving to the edge of her seat, "you all called this meeting, more so for Camille but she isn't the only one who's had to suffer.

Nonetheless, because you all suffered together, God is about to do a new thing, in this circle. He's about to birth, physically and spiritually, among you and just like the pain of birthing out a baby; you'll also endure the pain of pushing out your purpose. Camille, if you're ready to receive God, you can do it, right here and now. Are you ready?" she asks holding out her hand.

I finally take it and she stand, speaking in tongue. "God says, there's some more dark days coming but if you trust Him to do what He does, you'll make it. Great is thy faithfulness. Great is thy faithfulness. You are God's beloved and He's with you. Do you commit, by the words of your mouth that God is your savior and you want to be renewed?"

"I do?"

"Do you desire to place God back as the head of your life?"

"I do."

"Have you been baptized?"

"I have?"

"Then you are now recommitted to God," she tells me pulling me into a hug before she speaks in tongue again.

"Some of you will have to admit some mistakes of your past, some of you will face a loss and some of you will have to be in prayer like never before. Yes, it's going to be hard but you all can do it, or you wouldn't be sitting here."

Chapter 39

We're all crying and after a few minutes, Lyn asks a question.

"How do you know, for sure, if the thing you're trying to restore is the same as what God wants?"

"If it's God's doing, it'll be worth it but if its flesh, it'll be worrisome. If it's God, you'll get up ready to fight but if it isn't, you'll lay down wore out with no resolution. Yet, the best way to get clarity is fasting and praying." Pastor French tells her.

"Okay," Shelby sighs, "this is more personal but how do I know when it's the right time to move on? Will God show me?"

"He most definitely will," Rev. French replies. "Shelby, God knows everything we do, before we do it. Bible says, He knew us before we were formed in our mother's womb. Sweetie, you've gone through the unimaginable pain of losing a spouse and only you know when it's the right time to move on. Whether it's three months or three years, don't allow man's time table to dictate how and when you live. You are responsible for your own happiness."

"Yes ma'am."

"Whew," Kerri says, "I'm just taking all of this in, because right now, my life seems to be heading in the right direction. I've started to pray more and Mike and I are going to renew our vows in August."

"Renewal is always good," Pastor Reeves says.

"I'm with Kerri. Things are going good for my family and I've started to pray more. I didn't realize just how much difference it makes."

"Prayer has the ability to set the order of our day and life. Most think, praying the same thing over and over is fruitless but Bible tells us to never stop praying," Rev. French adds.

"Child, I'm taking life, minute by minute," Ray states. "Since the divorce from Justin, things have started to even out. More than anything, being back in church has helped me and the kids. Rashida is finally speaking to her dad again and I don't look at him with venom in my eyes, every time he comes to get them anymore," she laughs. "As for my personal life, Anthony and I are trying to see how things go. We're still in the dating phase and so far, we're enjoying it."

"Ladies, I wish finding a solution to every problem was as easy as calling a prayer meeting but truth is this life takes work. Yes, some of us face more hell, than others but it doesn't mean you cannot survive. You can heal, anything that you're strong enough to reveal. Why? Because you take back the power, the moment you give your pain a voice.

Let's pray.

Dear God, you've allowed us to gather here, in humble submission to you and for that we say, thank you. Thank you for giving us access to you because we know when we call, you have a responsibility to answer.

God, today we need you to hear and answer. For Camille, Shelby, Chloe, Kerri, Ray and Lyn; hear God.

But don't just hear, listen and respond. Their lives were turned upside down before but you allowed them to make it through then, do it again.

Bless now, each of these ladies. Some of them needs healing, some need confirmation, some need strength, some need to be restored and all need you. God, Rev. French and I, are simply your vessels and now that we've been obedient to you; you take over. Right any wrongs, oh God and hear from their heart.

God, we need you to deliver and set free. We need the enemy to know, today we're taking back the power because he doesn't have dominion over us. We're taking back our names, our homes, our marriages, our children and our sanity.

Today, we shall protect our joy and at this moment, we're snatching our lives back from the enemy. You've given us power and today, we're claiming it. We are powerful women of God and we will survive. The enemy will no longer dictate the rhythm to which we dance, because today, we're dancing to the sound of joy.

We thank you, God. We love you, God. We trust you, God because you've never failed us. No matter the many times we've ignored your call and failed you, you've never failed us. This is why, we'll press on. This is why, we'll hold on. Thank you God and we submit this prayer by faith, believing that it's already being worked out. Amen."

We all say amen before hugging Pastor Magnolia and Rev. French.

"Camille," Pastor Magnolia says pulling me to the side. "God says, He'll reveal your enemies but you need to be careful what you ask for. He also told me to tell you to say yes to Hagar."

"Hag—" I laugh and shake my head. "Yes ma'am."

"I'm here if and when you need me."

"Thank you."

Chapter 40

The next morning, I wake up to calls and texts from Carin.

I sit up in the bed and dial her number.

"Carin, hey this is Camille—"

"Look, I've been trying to reach you because your medical records have been released to the media."

"No," I say laying my head back, against the headboard. "Damn it."

"Don't worry, I have this taken care of but you're going to have to make a statement. Where are you?"

"I'm at home."

"Get dressed. I'll be there in an hour."

I press end on the phone and throw it, into the wall. It doesn't break but it dings with a notification.

I throw the covers back and get up to get it. Picking it up, I see a notification of a daily bible verse.

"Really God?"

I lean against the bed and click on it.

"Matthew ten, verse twenty-two," I read. *"You will be hated by everyone on account of My name but the one who perseveres to the end will be saved."*

"God, I don't understand but I'm willing. Forgive me for trying to do things on my own but I'm ready now. Ready to surrender to you. You said I had to be ready when you reveal my enemies, I'm there but please give me strength to endure. Amen."

A knock on the door.

"Camille—"

"Thomas, not now."

"I only came to apologize about last night and to see if I can take you and the kids to breakfast."

"Well, on an average day, going to breakfast with my husband and children, would be great. However, I'm getting ready to do an interview with a reporter because my medical records have been released. Oh and that video from last night. So, no thanks, I'll pass."

He exhales and closes the door.

Once done, in the bathroom and getting dressed, I stop by and ask TJ to meet me in Courtney's room. I explain to them what's happening and why. I didn't want them to have to hear about the overdose, on the news.

They took it better than I expected. I thought they'd be disappointed in me but instead, they embraced me.

An hour to the tee, Carin is ringing the doorbell. I didn't bother to ask how she got my address; it doesn't matter. Currently, I'm sitting in a chair, getting makeup done.

"Camille, listen. You will not deny having drugs in your system but you'll say, you were at a party, was given a drink that was laced with drugs."

"What about the 911 call? Won't they be able—"

"Girl, your name wasn't mentioned in that call and the ambulance transported you as an unknown black female. I told you, let me do my job."

I hold up my hands in defeat.

"You'll also be asked about your husband's affair, because of the video that was plastered to social media, last night. You can be frank, if you want or you don't have to tell them anything. If I see the interview going left, I'll pull the plug."

"Okay."

"Oh, whatever you do, do not lose your cool. This is you taking back your story. Do not, under any circumstances, allow them to dictate what you share and who you are. You are in control. Understood?"

"Got it," I tell her.

"Good, let's go."

"Wait, do you think this will kill my chance of getting the seat?"

"Hell no, I'm great at my job. All I need you to do, is do yours."

She walks off and thirty minutes later, I'm sitting in a chair, in the middle of my living room with a microphone clipped to my shirt and a camera in my face.

After the reporter does her introduction, she turns to me. "Mrs. Shannon, my name is Lauren Daniels. First, congratulations on your recent nomination to fill the seat, vacated by Judge Sumner."

"Thank you."

"I'm going to cut right to the chase. In light of the reports that we've received, concerning your medical history, do you really think you're capable of handling this position, if you were chosen?"

"Ms. Daniels, I've been preparing to become a judge since I was able to talk because law is all I've ever known and if you think for one moment, I'm going to allow someone, whomever it is that is leaking my personal information to stop that, I will not."

"That's all fine and good but according to this report you overdosed on a cocaine cocktail. Is that true?"

"Yes, in September 2018, I accidentally overdosed. It wasn't something I did on purpose but I was out, having a drink and my drink was spiked. I had no idea it was or what happened to me, until I woke up in the hospital, seven days later."

"I'm only wondering, how the citizens of District Seven will feel about you becoming their presiding judge when you have a history?"

"Ms. Daniels, don't we all have a history? What's to say your history is better than mine yet you're sitting here, judging me because mine has been made public?"

"It's my job," she states with an attitude.

"And when I'm chosen to fulfill the duties of District Seven it'll be my job and if you've done your due diligence then I'm sure you know how serious I take my job. Look, Ms. Daniels, I'm not perfect, never claimed to be but don't condemn me for making mistakes when I've yet to meet someone who doesn't make them either.

I get that I'll be working for the people but that still doesn't give the people, the power to determine my value. I'm a damn good attorney and I'll make an even better judge."

"What about your personal life?" she questions.

"What about it?"

"From a video that has been shared thousands of times on social media, it seems your husband has been unfaithful and has a baby on the way."

"It's true but he isn't the only one to fault for the damage in our marriage and while I could lie, I won't because my marriage isn't perfect. The young lady, in the video, claims to be pregnant by my husband and if that's true, will deal with it."

"Are you getting a divorce?"

"Truth is, Ms. Daniels I don't know what the future holds for me and my husband but what I do know, whether I'm married or divorced; it will not take away my knowledge and ability to practice law."

"Why should the people support you?" she questions.

"They should support me based on who I am now, my morals, my work history and not my mistakes. Ms. Daniels, I've made plenty of mistakes and will probably make more but I'll never let the people of District Seven down, on purpose. If I didn't think I was ready for this position, I would have turned it down, the minute I knew by name was submitted."

"Why didn't you? I mean, you had to know all these things would come out so why not take this time, get your life together and then run in an election?"

"My life is together," I correct. "Ms. Daniels, if you wake up one day with a, let's say, sore throat, does it stop you from going to work?"

"No but a sore throat isn't the same as a broken marriage."

"True but a sore throat means there's something wrong with you yet it doesn't stop you from working. Same for me. Yes, my marriage is in trouble and I've done some things but none of those prevent me from doing my job. Besides, I have to believe this is God's plan for me, at this very moment."

She chuckles, "people are good at calling on God when they're in trouble."

"You're right but the difference here, I called on God when I was in trouble then; I'm not in trouble now. At this moment, I'm being tested and I'm okay with that because it comes with purpose." I lean forward and clasp my hands together.

"Ms. Daniels, if I've learned anything, over this past year, it's that we can't stop God's plan for us and if He bought me this far, He'll see me through it. I don't know what's going to happen tomorrow or even next week but I can't worry about that.

My focus now is being a better person, continuing my therapy and fulfilling the requirements of my purpose. If taking over the seat of District Seven is part of the plan then I give God my full yes."

She's looking at me with wide eyes.

She clears her throat. "There you have it, citizens of Memphis. Is Camille Shannon the right woman for

District Seven? We'll find out when Governor Lee makes his final decision. This is Lauren Daniels reporting for Channel 2 News."

"Cut," a man says.

"I hope you don't think I was coming after you. I have to ask the tough questions."

"I understand," I tell her, standing to shake her hand.

"Congratulations again and I hope everything works out for you."

Chapter 41

When they leave, I sit on the couch with my phone in my hands. A few minutes later, I dial Dr. Scott's office.

"Yes, is Dr. Scott available?"

"May I ask who's calling?"

"Camille Shannon," I state.

"One moment."

"Mrs. Shannon, how may I help you?"

"I'm in, for the Hagar Experience; I'm in." I blurt before I change my mind, "but can it be this weekend?"

"Um," she says, sounding like she's flipping pages. "Yes, I am available. You will need to be here Friday evening because your session begins Saturday morning, at 8 AM. Check-out is Sunday at 3 PM. You will not have access to anybody and no phones. Are you committed to that?"

"Yes."

"Great, I'll email you all the details."

"Thank you."

I lay the phone on the table and get up to wash this makeup off my face when the doorbell rings.

I open it to find Lyn, whose eyes are red and puffy.

"Lyn, hey, come in. What's wrong?"

"Paul lied. He said Kandis wasn't pregnant but she is. He's a liar." I pull her into a hug.

I change clothes and fix Lyn and I some coffee before joining her in the living room.

"Here," I hand her the cup and sit next to her. "Tell me what happened?"

"I told you that Paul stood me up for dinner. Well that night, I went to his house and he gave me the excuse that his son was sick. Fine, I was mad but it is what it is but while talking to him, Kandis announced, she was pregnant again by Paul."

"That's why you left the country, right?"

"Yes, because I couldn't believe I'd been so stupid to let him in again. Anyway when I got back, he showed up at my apartment one night with food and we ended up sleeping together. He told me Kandis lied about being pregnant and they only co-parent together.

And like a fool, I believed him again. We've been hanging out, watching movies, going to dinner; everything. Yesterday, I had a doctor's appointment and," she sits the coffee down to reach into her purse, "I'm pregnant."

I take the ultrasound from her and I'm in a state of shock.

"I go to Paul's office to see if he wanted to do lunch so I can tell him and guess who shows up."

"Kandis," I say.

"Kandis with a belly that clearly shows she wasn't lying about being pregnant. Oh and here's the kicker, he proposed to her on Valentine's Day."

"That motherfucker," I say through clenched teeth.

She bursts into tears.

I sit my cup down and pull her into me.

"Sister, what is wrong with me?" she cries.

"Girl, there is absolutely nothing wrong with you. You're dealing with the cards, you've been dealt which includes a sorry ass man. You can't take the blame for what he's done but you can stop him from having access to you."

"Cam, I love that man. I've loved him since I was a teenager. He's the only man I've ever loved and for him to do this to me, again; I feel like I can't take anymore."

"Lynesha Williams, you listen to me." I push her up. "You are a damn good woman, mother, business owner and friend. You've been through some of the worst times, of your life yet, you're sitting right here. That makes you strong and you can take some more. Some more love, laughter, light and if God allows, you may see some more pain and suffering. Yet, don't ever think you can't survive it. Hell, look at me."

"I'm so tired Cam."

"I know baby but you have to make it, Lyn, for Kelsey and the life you have growing inside of you. Girl, you're damn near 40 and if God saw fit to impregnate you now, it's for a reason."

She looks at me and we both laugh.

"Lyn, you need to put some slack in the hold, you have on Paul. I know he's what you're used to and comfortable with and all the years you all spent together was good but it's time you let him go."

"You're right," she tells me wiping her face. "If I don't, he's going to be the death of me."

"And then I'll be the death of him."

"Thank you sister and I'm sorry for not calling before I came rushing over here."

"Whenever you need me, I'll always be here, whether you call or not. Now, what are you going to do about this baby?"

"I'm keeping it. Maybe this is God's plan for me to start over."

"Speaking of starting over, there's something I need to tell you. With everything you have going on this isn't how I planned to have this conversation but," I exhale, "when I was in law school, I was raped."

"What?" she asks with a shock look on her face. "You were—you never told me?"

I take her hand. "I'm sorry I never told you but in all fairness, I never told anybody. However, recently I've come to realize, the only way I can overcome this, I have to own it."

She stares at me, for a few seconds before pulling me into a hug.

"I know how devastating rape can be," she whispers, "but it doesn't have to be the end of you."

"And I know how devastating loss can be," I say to her, "but it doesn't have to be the end of you. Lyn, we have to survive this."

We stay that way, for a few minutes, not saying anything. Finally, we release each other.

"I'm going to a therapy retreat this weekend. I think it's what I need to do to finally heal. Why don't you come with me?" I ask her.

"Nah, I'm not ready to pour out my soul to a complete stranger. I'll be okay," she tells me.

"Are you still going to Maui?" I ask, walking her to the door.

"Yes, God knows I need that vacation and it'll be good to be surrounded by happiness, for a change. What about you? With everything going on, are you going to be able to make it?"

"Hell yes, my only dilemma is if I want to bring Thomas along. I'm hoping Governor Lee makes his announcement before we leave."

"You don't need no announcement to know, you got this."

"Thanks Lyn. You be careful and call me if you need me."

Chapter 42

A few days later, I'm at work, trying to get some things finished but I'm nervous about this therapy retreat, tomorrow.

I'm looking over the email from Dr. Scott and it says, I can arrive, either late tonight or by 7 AM, tomorrow morning. Good thing, it's only an hour away and I've already packed a small, overnight bag.

"Stephanie, can you pull the case file for Blake vs Crawley for me?"

"Sure thing, I will bring it right in."

Ten minutes later, Stephanie rushes in with the file and a look of excitement on her face.

"What?" I ask, looking at her.

"Governor Lee's office is on the line," she states bubbling with excitement.

"Really?"

"Yes, pick it up; pick it up."

"Okay, oh my God." I take a deep breath. "This is Camille Shannon."

"Please hold for Governor Lee."

"Mrs. Shannon, how are you today?"

"Governor Lee, I'm great sir. How are you?"

"Great. Listen, I won't hold you long but I wanted to call and officially offer you the seat of Circuit Court Judge District 7. I cannot lie and say I wasn't disturbed by the recent events, in the news but I'm very impressed by your qualifications and the way you've handled your shortcomings.

Young lady, there were a lot of obstacles created to try and keep you from this position which lets me know, you're the one I need in this seat. I know you will serve it well. Don't disappoint me."

"I won't sir and thank you for giving me a chance."

"The official announcement will be released within the hour and later, someone from my office will call with the official swearing in and other details. Congratulations Mrs. Shannon."

"Thank you, sir."

"Oh my God Stephanie," I scream as she begins jumping up and down. "Can you please get my husband on the line?"

Mr. Townsend and Carin walk into my office with champagne.

"I should have known you would already know."

"The press kits have already started going out. Congratulations Camille." Carin says.

"I am so proud of you Camille." Mr. Townsend says coming over to give me a hug.

"I couldn't have done this without both of you. Especially you, Mr. Townsend. Thank you for believing in me."

"Always have and I won't stop now."

"Cam, your husband is on line one."

I step over to my desk, "hey, I wanted to call you to let you know, I got the seat."

"I had no doubt that you would. Congratulations but can I call you right back?"

"Seriously?"

"I was in the middle of something—" I hang up on him.

Taking a few deep breaths, I dial my dad's office. When he answers, I squeal into the phone, "daddy," I say with tears streaming down my face.

"I already know baby girl and your mother and I are so very proud of you. She's already looking for flights to fly into Memphis," he laughs.

"Oh my God, this doesn't feel real."

"It is and you may as well get ready. I can hear the noise in your office so you go on and enjoy this moment. I love you. Call us when you make it home."

I hang up and go into the bathroom to get myself together. Coming back to my desk, I send a group text out to the girls and then make my way over to some of the associates and coworkers, who are there.

I spend some time thanking everybody before going back over to Carin and Mr. Townsend.

"How does it feel?" he questions.

"It hasn't sunk in yet."

"Well get ready because from here, things will move fast. The swearing in, will mostly likely take place in two weeks. You'll be sent all the details so that you can invite your family and friends." Carin says as I feel someone come up behind me.

"Thomas," I say throwing my arms around his neck. "You came?"

"You know I wouldn't have missed this. Regardless of what we've been through, I'm so proud of you," he says sweeping me up into a hug.

"Thank you," I say hugging him extra tight.

He shakes hands with Mr. Townsend and I introduce him to Carin, my publicist.

"Mr. Townsend it is nice to see you again sir and Carin it's nice to meet you. I am sure you're preparing for all of the news trucks that I saw pulling up outside."

"The real fun begins now," she says, "but you let me handle that. You enjoy the celebration."

Judge Alton walks in with a few of the other partners and associates offering their congratulations.

"Judge Alton, thank you for coming." I say as he gives me a hug.

"I wouldn't have missed it. Congratulations, Mrs. Shannon."

"Everybody grab a glass," Mr. Townsend announces. "To Camille, we here at Townsend and Associates couldn't be prouder of you, for all you've accomplished. I have no doubt you'll make one hell of a judge because you've never wavered at being an attorney. We raise our glass to you today and please know we love you here and will always have your back. To Judge Camille."

"Judge Camille!"

Thomas turns and kisses me. We stay in the office celebrating for the next hour.

"Let's get out of here," Thomas whispers in my ear.

Making it to Thomas' truck, he has a huge smile. "What are you up too?"

"It's a surprise."

"Wait, what about my car? I need it."

"We'll come back and get it, later."

I start to say something but don't. He opens the door and I get in with no idea what he could have planned so quickly. We don't drive far before getting to a boat dock, at the river. He pulls in and park.

I look at him and he opens his door.

"Good evening, I am Isaac and we have everything taken care of for you. Right this way," I hear him say.

"Thank you, Isaac." Thomas says, coming around to open my door.

"Stop trying to figure it out Camille and just follow Isaac."

"Wow! This is beautiful," I say stepping onto one of the largest boats I've ever seen. It was decked out on the inside. I mean absolutely amazing. "And it smells great in here."

"That would be thanks to our chef for tonight."

"Please don't tell it's Chelle."

"Really Camille?"

I shrug.

"Good evening Judge Shannon."

Chapter 43

"Todd?"

He moves and I see, Chloe, Ray, Shelby, Kerri, Mike, Lyn and Anthony.

"Oh my God! How?" I say, as the tears start.

"Your husband with the help of Anthony and Ray, pulled all of this together in less than an hour," Shelby tells me.

"Just a way to congratulate you on becoming Judge Camille Shannon. We are proud of you girl." Ray says smiling.

"Y'all," I pause, "I could not have done this without your support. When I didn't believe in myself, you all did. When I was losing myself, you all wouldn't let me die. Y'all love me, flaws and all and, whew," I say, fanning my face to keep from crying. "I don't know what lies ahead, on this new journey but I need each by my side. I love you guys."

"We love you too. Let's eat!"

After eating and doing a little dancing, I pull Lyn to the side.

"Hey, you okay?"

"Yes girl, I'm good."

"The baby?" I whisper.

"So far, everything is good. I haven't talked to Paul since the day at his office and I don't know if I am."

"Have you told anybody else?"

"Not yet," she says looking at the girls. "I'm only eight weeks and trying to come to terms with things, first."

"I got you boo but don't shut me out this time."

"I won't."

I give her a hug.

"What are you heifers whispering about?" Ray questions.

"Nothing sister. Turn this music up and let's dance."

*****

After spending a few hours, celebrating, we finally make it home. I check in on the kids who were asleep and for once in a long time, I truly enjoyed hanging with my husband.

Getting ready to walk into the guestroom, Thomas pulls me in our bedroom.

He kisses me and I smile.

"Thank you for an amazing night," I tell him.

"You deserved it."

"I don't know about that," I say removing my jacket. "Babe, I know things have been rough, between us and I am truly sorry for everything I've done. This last year and a half, has been draining and you were right."

"About what?" he asks.

"Me needing to fight for you."

"Camille—"

"No, you've always fought for me, the many times you should have kicked my ass out but you didn't. Even after everything, you pulled together a party to celebrate me when you should have run off into the sunset with Chelle. God knows, she's probably paid you more attention, in the short amount of time you've known her, than I have this past year.

Just know, I'm sorry and I'm vowing to be a better person," I exhale. "With the help of Dr. Scott and this therapy weekend, I'm going to find me again."

"Are you sure this weekend is the right time, after being selected for the seat?"

"Thomas, it's even more reason, along with me wanting to be better for you and the kids. You all deserve me whole because you've spent, far too long, dealing with the broke me. That's if you still want me."

He leans in to kiss me and I let our tongues connect, kissing this man like it's the last time I'll ever taste him because I've missed him, in my soul.

He steps back and I move to unbutton his shirt but he grabs my hand.

"Babe, there's something we need to talk about, first. Well, something I need to tell you."

"Can it wait? Let's just enjoy tonight and we can talk about whatever else when I get home."

"I wish it could but it can't. Come and sit with me." He leads me to the sitting area, of the bedroom and begins to pace.

"Thomas, what is it? You're scaring me. What's going on?"

"When you finally admitted to cheating, on me, I wasn't shocked because I'd seen the signs. I ignored them because you were my wife and I love you. Then things started to get progressively worse. You started being unapologetic about everything, not caring who you hurt in the process."

"What—"

He holds up his hand and I stop.

"After the overdose, I'd decided I didn't want to be married to you anymore and as soon as you were well, I was going to file for divorce. Until I saw you changing and the person I fell in love with, was starting to show up, again. I knew I couldn't let you go. All I wanted was you but then this seat came open, in the district and you were nominated."

"Thomas, what are you getting at?"

"I was angry because instead of you, taking the time to work on us, you were putting yourself into another position where I'd have to share you."

"Share me?"

"Yes," he yells but then takes a deep breath. "I'm sick of sharing you with everybody so I---"

"You what?" I ask with confusion.

"It was me," he whispers.

"It was you what?" I ask getting angry.

"It was me," he pauses again, "I leaked your files to the media."

Although this book is fiction, there are a lot of women and men, who find themselves being shattered by things of the past. If by chance this book has triggered unresolved emotions, for you, I pray that your faith doesn't fail.

If you're in the need of prayer, you can email me at authorlakisha@gmail.com. If you're in need of counseling, don't hesitate, out of fear, of getting the help you need.

Therapy isn't a bad thing.

Thank you for taking the time to support my work. I hope you've enjoyed the first book, of the Shattered Series which is a revision of Ms. Nice Nasty. As of now this series will be three books with part 2, being Cam's Confession.

Be on the lookout for it, in the coming weeks and then the finale.

My prayer is that you've enjoyed the revision of Ms. Nice Nasty into Shattered. If you did, please share it, shout it out on social media and tag me.

Happy Reading.

Lakisha

About the Author

Lakisha Johnson, native Memphian and author of over fifteen titles was born to write. She'll tell you, "Writing didn't find me, it's was engraved in my spirit during creation." Along with being an author, she is an ordained minister, co-pastor, wife, mother and the product of a large family.

She is a blogger at kishasdailydevotional.com and social media poster where she utilizes her gifts to encourage others to tap into their God given talents. She won't claim to be the best at what she does nor does she have all the answers; she is simply grateful to be used by God.

Again, I thank you for taking the time to read my work! I cannot express what it means to me every time you support me! If this is your first time reading my work, please check out the many other books available by visiting my Amazon Page.

For upcoming contests and give-a-ways, I invite you to like my Facebook page, AuthorLakisha, follow my blog https://authorlakishajohnson.com/ or join my reading group Twins Write 2.

Or you can connect with me on Social Media.

Twitter: _kishajohnson | Instagram: kishajohnson | Snapchat: Authorlakisha

Email: authorlakisha@gmail.com

Also available

When the Vows Break

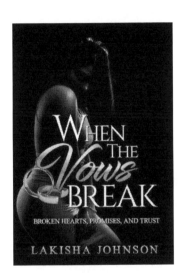

Dearly beloved, that's how it begins, what God has joined together, let no man put asunder; that's how it ends. Happily married, wedded bliss and with these rings, we do take; but what happens to happily ever after when the vows break?

Secrets, lying, cheating, drugs, alcohol and temptations prove that not everything is what it seems. Will the chaos of it all be more than they can take? Find out in part 1 of When the Vows Break

Broken

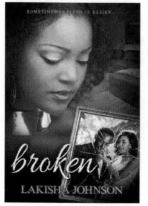

Gwendolyn was 13 when her dad shattered her heart, leaving her broken. Her mother told her, a daddy can break a girl's heart before any man has a chance and she was right.

Through many failed relationships and giving herself to any man who showed interest, she knew she had to get herself together. So, she gave up on men.

Until Jacque. He came into her life with promises to love, honor and cherish her; forsaking all others until death do, they part. Twelve years later, he has made good on his promises until he didn't.

The Family that Lies:

Forsaken by Grayce, Saved by Merci

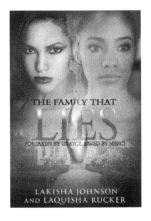

While Grayce got love and attention, Merci got all the hell, forcing her to leave home. She never looks back, putting the past behind her until ... her sister shows up over a decade later begging for help, bringing all of the forgotten past with her. Merci wasn't the least bit prepared for what was about to happen next.

Merci realizes, she's been a part of something much bigger than she'd ever imagined. Yea, every family has their secrets, hidden truths and ties but Merci had no idea she'd been born into the family that lies.

The Family that Lies: Merci Restored

In the Family that Lies: Merci Restored, we revisit the Alexanders to see how life has treated them. Three years ago, Merci realized she'd been a part of something much bigger than she ever could have imagined. Sure, every family has their secrets, hidden truths and ties but Merci had no idea she'd been born into the family that lies ... without caring who it hurts!

Now, years later, Merci finds herself in the midst of grief, a new baby and marriage while still learning how to pick up the broken pieces of her life.

All while Melvin is still raising hell!

In this special edition of The Family that Lies, there will be questions answered and new drama but I have to warn you ... there will also be tragedy, hurt and of course LIES!

The Pastor's Admin

DISCLAIMER This is Christian FICTION which includes some sex scenes and language. ***

Daphne 'Dee' Gary used to love being an admin ... until Joseph Thornton.

Joseph is the founder and pastor of Assembly of God Christian Center and he is, hell, there are so many words Daphne can use to describe him but none are good. He does things without thinking of the consequence because he knows Dee will be there to bail him out. Truth is, she has too because ... it's her job, right? A job she has been questioning lately.

Daphne knows life can be hard and flesh will sometimes win but when she has to choose between HIS SECRETS or HER SANITY, this time, will she remain The Pastor's Admin?

The Marriage Bed

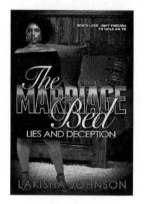

Lynn thinks their marriage bed is suffering and wants to spice it up. Jerome, on the other hand, thinks Lynn is overreacting. His thoughts, if it ain't broke, don't break it trying to fix it. Then something happens that shakes up the Watson household and secrets are revealed but the biggest secret, Jerome has and his lips are sealed.

Bible says in Hebrews 13:4, "Let marriage be held in honor among all and let the marriage bed be undefiled, for God will judge the sexually immoral and adulterous." But what happens when life starts throwing daggers, lies, turns and twists?

Still Fighting: My sister's fight with Trigeminal Neuralgia

Still Fighting is an inside look into my sister's continued fight with Trigeminal Neuralgia, a condition known as the Suicide Disease because of the lives it has taken. In this book, I take you on a journey of recognition, route and restoration from my point of view; a sister who would stop at nothing to help her twin sister/best friend fight to live.

It is my prayer you will be blessed by my sister's will to fight and survive.

The Forgotten Wife

All Rylee wants is her husband's attention.

She used to be the apple of Todd's eye but no matter what she did, lately, he was just too busy to notice her. She could not help but wonder why.

Then one day, an unexpected email, subject line: Forgotten Wife and little did she know, it was about to play a major part in her life.

They say first comes love then comes ... a kidnapping, attacks, lies and affairs. Someone is out for blood but who, what when and why?

Secrets are revealed and Rylee fears for her life when all she ever wanted was not to be The Forgotten Wife.

Other Available Titles

A Compilation of Christian Stories: Box Set

Dear God: Hear My Prayer

2:32 AM: Losing My Faith in God

When the Vows Break 2

When the Vows Break 3

Bible Chicks: Book 2

Doses of Devotion

You Only Live Once: Youth Devotional

HERoine Addict – Women's Journal

Be A Fighter - Journal

Made in the USA
Middletown, DE
06 November 2019